JUST A LITTLE PROMISE

NEW YORK TIMES BESTSELLING AUTHORS

Carly Phillips

Erika Wilde

He's the one she's never forgotten.
She's the one he regrets letting go.
Now they have a second chance to get it right.

When Skye Tremont runs into her sexy former flame, Tripp Daniels, she's reminded of the baby pact they'd made years ago… If she was single and childless by the age of thirty, he'd step in and be her baby daddy and fulfill her dream of having a child.

Now, after a bitter divorce that has left her guarding her heart, and wanting only one thing, Skye is ready to take Tripp up on his promise. When he's one of the bachelors up for bid at a charity auction, it's the perfect opportunity to have him all to herself for a weekend of baby making fun, as long as he agrees to her terms.

Tripp is on board to fulfill the promise he made to Skye. If he's going to have a baby with anyone, it's going to be the one woman he'd foolishly let slip through his fingers. But not this time because he's all in. Skye is even more beautiful than he remembers, and the chemistry between them is hotter than ever, but while she gives him free rein with her body, she's made it clear her heart is off limits.

Now, with a second chance within his grasp, Tripp is prepared to do whatever it takes to win the woman he loves and give them both the family they've always craved.

Chapter One

"COME ON. ONE last round, and this time show me what you've really got."

Skye Abbott heard her brother's encouraging voice but kept her focus on the punching bag he held in place for her to pummel. With every solid, direct hit she took, she imagined her ex's smug, pretentious face.

Punch, punch, kick.

She'd been at today's kickboxing session for nearly half an hour and felt the burn in her core and every other muscle in her body. Sweat beaded on her skin, and her ponytail smacked her back and shoulders with each jab at her target.

Punch, punch, kick.

The adrenaline rush was exhilarating. As was the capable, confident, empowered feeling coursing through her—all the things her ex had methodically stripped from her during the course of their marriage.

Piece by piece, she'd managed to rebuild her confidence and self-worth, and swore she'd never let herself be that vulnerable again. She ended the round with one final *punch, punch, kick, punch, punch.*

"Good job," Spencer said, releasing the bag and

grinning at her. "You were a savage today, sis."

Still breathing hard, she took off her boxing gloves and accepted the bottle of water he held out to her. "That's because I have an excellent coach."

Spencer had encouraged her to give kickboxing a try when she'd moved to New York four months ago, after her divorce had been finalized. Not only did he want her to build her strength but also to make sure she had some form of self-defense to fall back on should the need arise.

"Well, you've come a long way from your first session," he said with a laugh.

She chugged half the bottle of water, remembering that day so well. How timid she'd been. Her weak, uncertain punches. Feeling so uncoordinated and awkward. But Spencer had been relentless in his training, demanding she hit harder, faster, and beat the shit out of the bag like her life depended on it.

She appreciated his tough love approach, and gradually, over the past few months she felt her mind and body repairing itself and her return to the old Skye, the one she'd been before she'd met Jack Tremont. After four hellish years, it was as though she'd finally emerged from the stifling cloak of darkness and back into the light.

"So, any plans for tonight?" she asked as she wiped the sweat from her face and neck with a small towel she'd left on a nearby bench.

"Yep." He glanced at her as they left the gym located in his apartment building and headed for the elevator. "Got a date."

He waggled his brows, and since said date came without a name, Skye knew that it was probably just one of the casual hook-ups from his "Little Black Book" app. With his sandy blond hair, deep blue eyes, and flirtatious nature, along with being a stockbroker on Wall Street, there was no shortage of women vying for his attention. But her brother was an unapologetic bachelor through and through.

"Want me to find somewhere else to crash for the night?" *Like a hotel room.* She was starting to feel guilty about living at his place, and therefore hindering his ability to "entertain", *aka have sex with*, those dates at home. And the last thing she wanted was to hear her brother in the room next to hers, doing *that.*

He shook his head and punched the button for the elevator, which immediately opened for them to step inside. "No, I can make other arrangements."

Which he'd been doing for the past four months. "I'm cramping your style," she said, and sighed. "I really need to find a place of my own."

"I told you, there's no rush," he said, and she heard the protective tone in his voice. "I want you to feel settled before—"

"I venture out on my own in big, bad New York City?" she finished for him, albeit sarcastically.

His lips pursed in annoyance. "Yes."

The elevator opened on his floor and she followed him to his apartment, then inside, while arguing her point. "It's been four months since I moved here and it's time. You can't protect me forever."

"I'm your big brother," he said, turning to face her and placing his hands on her shoulders. "It's my job to be overbearing and protective."

She saw the pained look in his eyes, and knew the source. He'd worn that same expression the day she'd finally found the courage to leave Jack, and Spencer had picked her up, bringing her to her parent's home with one suitcase holding all her meager possessions. He'd already been furious with her husband for his mental and emotional abuse, but Spencer had taken one look at her, and his anger had dissolved into guilt, because he hadn't realized how bad things had become. Especially when she told him that Jack had finally crossed a line and hit her.

Like other women in her position, she'd become good at making excuses about not seeing her family, and perfecting ways to fake being happy when the reality was, she'd been miserable and controlled by a man who had gradually destroyed her resistance, her morale, and her spirit. And while her family had suspected that her marriage was not what she attempted to portray, they hadn't been prepared for the broken woman who'd walked into their house two years ago, a shell of her former self.

She was grateful for their support, the way they'd rallied around her and built her back up when she thought she'd never feel whole again. But now, she needed to take the next step in her life, without being swaddled like a newborn baby.

"I feel good, Spencer," she said, setting her boxing gloves and bottle of water on the table. "Really good. Stronger and better than I have in years. But I need my space and independence back so I can start planning my future. I've got a job that I love and the next step is finding a place of my own." She refrained from pointing out that she was thirty years old and didn't need his permission, because she knew his concern came from a place of love.

He was still wearing that unconvinced frown, stubborn as ever. "You're the one who encouraged me to move to New York in the first place," she reminded him.

"So you didn't have to deal with, or run into, that asshole you were married to in Boston," he grumbled.

"It's been five months since he signed the divorce papers," she said. Although he'd dragged his feet for over a year and a half, despite her wanting nothing from him except to cut all ties. "He's finally moving on, and I need to do the same."

The tense set of Spencer's shoulders relaxed a bit at her words. "Fine," he huffed. "We'll look at places together. I want final approval on your apartment building. There needs to be top notch security and a guard at the front desk."

She rolled her eyes, smiling at him. "If that makes you feel better."

He nodded his head decisively. "It will."

Giving him that peace of mind was the least she could do.

✧   ✧   ✧

SKYE SAT OUT on the tiny balcony of her new apartment, drinking her morning cup of coffee and enjoying the peaceful Saturday solitude. Well, the place wasn't so recent now that she'd been there for the past six months. But it still felt exciting and fresh to her, since it was the first place where she'd lived alone since leaving her ex-husband. She'd gone from staying with her parents, to being roommates with her brother, and she couldn't deny that the freedom of truly being on her own was liberating.

The Brooklyn apartment was a small two bedroom, but it had all the amenities she needed, and most importantly, it had received Spencer's seal of approval. It was in a nice neighborhood, and the security in the lobby was vigilant about letting in strangers and visitors. The location was top notch, with nearby markets and restaurants, and Prospect Park was within walking distance.

It was quiet here, unlike the hustle and bustle of New York City where she worked at the Meridian Hotel as an assistant event coordinator.

It was also the perfect place to raise a child.

The thought brought a smile to her lips as she took another drink of her coffee. Now that her marriage was officially over and far behind her, having a baby on her own had been on her mind. A lot. When she'd married Jack, it had been with the intention of starting a family, something she'd dreamed of since she was a little girl. She'd always imagined having an adoring husband, a house in the suburbs with the proverbial white picket fence, and at least three kids by the time she was thirty.

Jack had destroyed those hopes and dreams right along with her self-esteem, though a part of her was grateful that they hadn't had any kids which would have tied her to her ex for the rest of the children's lives. She shuddered at the thought.

She'd managed to rebuild her confidence, had a place of her own, and was finally in a good mental space to look toward the future. She might not trust her heart and emotions when it came to men—hell, she wasn't even interested in casually dating—but these days, women didn't need a man to have or raise a child. That's what sperm banks were for.

It was Saturday, and while she needed to do laundry and go to the market to pick up a few things for the following week, she had nothing planned for the afternoon and evening. So, she texted Lauren—her co-worker, who'd also become a good friend—to see if she wanted to meet for drinks and appetizers at The Back Door, a bar they'd been to a few times for happy hour after work. It meant taking an Uber into the city because no way was she stepping foot on the subway after dark.

Lauren responded with a quick and enthusiastic, *let's do it.* They agreed on six pm, before the place became too crowded on a Saturday night.

Opting for black skinny jeans, a loose fitting, short

sleeved blouse, and her favorite pair of red heels, Skye walked into the establishment right on time and saw Lauren already sitting at the bar, chatting with Raven, the female bartender serving drinks. She made her way over to her friend and slid into the vacant seat beside her.

"Hey," Lauren said by way of greeting, a smile on her pink, glossy lips. Normally, she wore her shoulder length bob straight, but today she'd added soft waves to the dark brown strands, giving her a sultrier look than her normal work appearance. "Sorry I didn't wait out front for you. I thought I'd grab us a few chairs before there weren't any left."

"Good idea." Skye placed her purse on a hook beneath the bar and settled in. They perused the happy hour menu for a few minutes, then placed their order when the bartender, Raven, came back around.

"What can I get for you ladies?" she asked, placing cocktail napkins on the bar top in front of them.

"I'll take your grilled chicken skewers with sweet potato fries and one of your Ruby Red Cosmos," Skye said, handing the menu back to Raven.

Lauren nodded. "That sounds good. I'll have the same. Make that two."

"Be right back with your drinks," Raven promised, then left them to place their appetizer orders.

Once they were alone, Lauren glanced at Skye with a mischievous look in her eyes. "So, did you happen to see the men in the bachelor auction brochure that will be up for bid at the Future Fast Track charity event next weekend?" She reached into her purse and withdrew a glossy booklet. "Billie dropped them off yesterday and I grabbed one on the way out the door," she said of the young woman who worked with the non-profit organization, dedicated to helping foster kids as they aged out of the system.

Skye and Lauren worked together at the Meridian NYC hotel as event coordinators—Lauren as lead, and Skye as her assistant. With their boss, Jade Dare, out on maternity leave, the two of them were now in charge of handling the upcoming gala. It was Skye's first big event, and she was both excited and nervous about how it was all going to come together. She'd only been with the Meridian for nine months, and more than anything, she wanted to make a good impression on both Lauren and Jade.

She'd seen the brochures when she'd left work the previous afternoon, but hadn't been at all tempted to grab one, not even to idly browse through.

"No, I didn't look," she replied to Lauren's question as Raven placed a pale pink drink in front of each of them. "After my divorce, the last thing I'm in the market for is a man. Well, except for maybe his swimmers," she added humorously.

Lauren had just taken a drink of her cocktail and choked on the liquid. She coughed, her eyes wide as she stared at Skye. "Care to explain *that* comment?"

Skye merely grinned and more carefully took a sip of her own Cosmo.

Lauren made an exasperated sound. "You can't

leave me dangling on such an intriguing comment. Are you insinuating that you're thinking about getting artificially inseminated?"

"Yes, and I'm beyond the thinking stage." Raven came by with their appetizers and Skye waited for the other woman to deliver the plates, then be on her way again before continuing. "I've already looked into it, and have even seen a reproductive endocrinologist in the city."

Her desire to have a child wasn't a secret. Her parents, Spencer, and even her other brother, Reese, knew and supported her decision to be a single mother, and understood why she'd decided to do this on her own. She wasn't in the market to get remarried anytime soon, and, well, her biological clock was ticking.

Her family just wasn't aware that she was *actively* trying to select a donor, and she didn't plan on telling them until she'd been inseminated and knew she'd actually conceived. The last thing she wanted was the stress of her mother constantly asking if she was pregnant yet. Since Reese and Spencer were still single and enjoying the bachelor life, their mother was anxious for Skye to provide that first grandchild her parents wanted so badly.

"Wow." Lauren popped a fry into her mouth, then tipped her head curiously. "So, how does the whole sperm selection thing work?"

"Well, everything is anonymous in terms of the donor's identity," Skye said, sharing what she'd already learned as she ate bites of her chicken. "I've been looking through profiles online, and they all include health history and genetic testing and screening. Then there's the person's physical attributes such as hair and eye color and height, and their heritage, educational background, and personality type. A lot of donors provide a baby picture of them at about a year old, to give you a general idea of what your child could potentially look like."

Lauren's eyes were filled with wonder. "It's amazing that women these days can hand pick their very own baby daddy. Are you looking for any particular features?"

Skye shrugged. "Not as much as I want to make sure the baby is healthy."

Okay, that wasn't completely true. Of course she wanted a healthy infant, but when she closed her eyes and imagined her child, she saw dark brown hair and green eyes. She envisioned a little boy who reminded her of Tripp Daniels, the one guy in her past that she'd never been able to forget . . . even if he'd shattered a piece of her heart with his inability to be more than friends with benefits. He'd ended things between them because he'd been far more focused on his schooling and career as a pediatric surgeon and had easily, she thought, walked away from what the two of them could have been.

Despite the fact that the relationship was long over, he'd been in her thoughts often lately, especially during this sperm donor selection process because of the silly promise he'd made her years ago. When she'd

CARLY PHILLIPS & ERIKA WILDE

told him that she'd wanted three kids by the time she was thirty, he'd given her his patented, charming grin and told her that if she was single and childless by that age, he'd be happy to give her a baby.

Yes, he'd been teasing her, but his promise lingered, as did memories of her time with Tripp—which had been *so good* until she'd made the mistake of asking for a commitment, when he'd made it clear from the start that he hadn't been looking for anything serious. But she'd gotten to a point where she wanted and needed more from their relationship and while she'd fallen in love with him, he clearly hadn't been in the same headspace.

He'd told her he was too focused on his pediatric surgical residency and still had a few more years to go to get certified, which meant a lot of long days and nights ahead and sacrificing a personal life. Then he'd ended things, telling her he wasn't anywhere near ready to settle down. So, they'd gone their separate ways, and a few months after breaking up with her, Skye had met Jack and her own life had changed, and not for the better.

Though she'd been tempted to search her new social media account just to see where his own life had taken Tripp, she'd refrained. That ship had sailed, and she wasn't the same gregarious woman she'd been back then. Life had changed her and she had no idea if he'd even like the cautious, more guarded woman she'd become.

Realizing she'd gotten lost in her thoughts, she

glanced back at Lauren, who'd finished her appetizers and was flipping through the bachelor auction brochure and reading the profiles. Interestingly enough, she'd even earmarked a few pages.

"So, what made you grab that bachelor auction brochure," Skye asked, pushing her own half-eaten plate of food to the side. "Curiosity, or something more?"

Lauren met her gaze and grimaced. "Something more, I'm afraid."

That piqued Skye's interest, and wanting a distraction from the memories of the past, she grinned at her friend. "Oh, do tell."

Lauren blew out a breath, a pained look in her eyes. "Well, my sister's wedding is coming up and she's marrying my ex, so I was thinking of taking a plus one to the event so I wouldn't be dateless and look pathetic. Except I don't have a plus one in my life, so . . . bidding on a bachelor for a weekend might be the solution to my problem."

Skye shook her head, trying to process the first part of what Lauren had just said. "Wait, I'm still hung up on the fact that your sister is marrying your *ex*."

Lauren laughed, but there was no real humor in the sound. "It's awkward, for sure, but . . . I'm fine, really."

Skye heard the reluctance in her friend's voice and didn't press for more details. She wasn't one to push or pry. Not when she had her own secrets she preferred to keep to herself.

"I have a week to decide if bidding on a stranger is the way to go," Lauren said, tucking the brochure back into her purse before smiling at Skye. "But at least I know I have options."

Skye nodded in understanding.

They decided to order one more drink and spent the next hour chatting about inconsequential things, like work and the upcoming charity event. They laughed about their favorite comedic show, dished about Taylor Swift's newest love interest, and shared their love for steamy romance novels, along with their favorite authors.

With their Cosmos finished and the bar area getting more crowded, they settled their tabs and prepared to leave, but before Skye slid off her chair, Lauren placed her hand on Skye's arm, stopping her.

"Hey, since it's a Saturday night, want to hit up Club Ten29?" Lauren asked.

Skye had heard of the trendy NYC nightclub, though she'd never been there. Dance clubs were not her thing, with the loud, vibrating music and crush of people. And the thought of getting hit on by strange men, and fending off their advances, was enough to make her shudder.

She smiled, hoping she didn't disappoint Lauren too much. "I think I'm just going to go home and read a book and relax."

Lauren thought for a moment, then nodded. "Actually, that doesn't sound like such a bad idea. I just didn't want you to think I was a boring date."

Skye laughed. "Trust me, *I'm* the boring one."

She grabbed her purse from beneath the bar and stood up, then turned to head toward the exit—too abruptly, she realized, as she bumped into a hard, broad chest. She stumbled back on her heels, and stiffened as two big hands gripped her arms and kept her from falling on her ass.

She managed to stifle the initial jolt of panic that shot through her at being grabbed so unexpectedly— PTSD at its finest, thanks to Jack—and blurted out an apology while staring at the man's throat.

"I'm so sorry, I wasn't paying attention—"

"Skye."

The man said just one word—her name—and his deep, husky voice stirred something intimately familiar inside of her. She jerked her head back and looked into seductive green eyes she'd never believed she'd see again.

As if her thoughts had conjured him, Tripp Daniels stood in front of her, a sexy smile quirking up the corners of his lips. Her breath left her lungs in a rush as she stared at his handsome face in wide-eyed shock, which quickly gave way to something she hadn't felt in a very long time. Years, in fact.

Undeniable desire.

Instantaneous attraction.

It all came flooding back, nearly overwhelming her, as if they'd never parted ways. The heat of his hands on her arms spread through her and the gentle sweep of his thumbs on her bare skin made her shiver with pleasure.

It was all she could do to keep her composure.

Still stunned and flustered at their unexpected run-in, all she could manage was a squeaky, high-pitched, awkward, "Hi!"

So much for being cool, calm, and collected.

Chapter Two

LIGHT, FEMALE LAUGHTER grabbed Tripp's attention and made him turn his head, but it was the woman's familiar profile that kept him riveted. Silky blonde hair cascaded down her back in soft waves as she chatted with the woman seated next to her, revealing a delicate silhouette he'd memorized years ago as she'd slept peacefully beside him. Right before he'd made the decision to break things off with her.

The slightly upturned nose, elegant cheekbones, and the sensual curve of her full lips. Yeah, those features were still emblazoned in his mind, no matter how hard he'd tried to forget her.

Or maybe he was just projecting what he *wanted* to see.

Was it Skye? Doubtful. Last he knew, she was living in Boston with her husband, probably with the three kids she'd wanted, and living a charmed life. Because seriously, what were the chances that they'd end up crossing paths in one of the hundreds of bars in New York City after five long years?

But the more he looked and watched her, he caught little quirks that were uniquely Skye's. He recognized the way she dipped her head when she laughed, and those cute, fluttering hand gestures she made when she was trying to describe something.

Holy shit, *it was her.*

"You keep staring at that woman at the bar like you want to eat her for dessert," Tripp's friend said, his tone both amused and intrigued. "Maybe you should before I do."

Tripp finally looked away from Skye and glanced back at Hudson, who was also his business partner. They'd decided to come here for drinks and appetizers after a long day at the Children's Community Clinic, where they'd spent the afternoon giving much needed vaccinations to children of low income families. It was something they did every other month—along with their other partner, Brett—donating their time and the cost of the various immunizations to help families without health insurance.

Tripp didn't miss the interest in Hudson's eyes. Even at forty-eight, he was still a good-looking guy. He had that whole distinguished, graying at the temples thing going for him, at least according to Amy, their receptionist. Hudson worked out daily and he was also charming and charismatic when he wanted to be. Now that he was divorced, Hudson didn't hesitate to play the field and he seemed to have an eye for the younger ladies. Blondes, especially. Which was why he was not-so-subtly expressing interest in Skye.

Tripp found himself bristling, which was ridiculous considering he had no right to be possessive of a long ago ex. Besides, as far as he knew, Skye wasn't single or available.

"Actually, I know her," he admitted to his friend.

Hudson's brows raised high. "And you're still sitting here with me when you could be with someone like *her* for the night?" he asked incredulously. "I mean, if you're not interested—"

"She's married," Tripp said pointedly, knowing that was one line his friend would never cross.

Hudson glanced back at Skye and stared at her for a moment before saying, "Are you sure about that? I don't see a ring on her finger."

Tripp turned his head back to Skye so quickly, he almost gave himself whiplash. He watched and waited for her to lift her left hand, and sure enough, it was completely bare, which really didn't prove or disprove her marital status. But if Skye was *Tripp's* wife, he knew for damn sure he'd make certain she wore her wedding ring while out at a bar without him so guys would think twice before hitting on her. So every man in the place would know she was his.

But she hadn't been his in years. And now, at the age of thirty-six, he could honestly say that letting her go was one of the biggest regrets of his adult life—even if he believed he'd been doing the right thing at the time.

"So, *how* do you know her?" Hudson asked curiously.

He drank the last of his bourbon before replying. "We met while I was living in Boston and attending

BU Med, and we dated for a few months."

Six months, actually—far longer than he'd ever intended to let things go on with Skye. At the time, he'd been all about casual hook-ups and one night stands because of his intense work and school schedule, but one taste of Skye and he'd been addicted to everything about her.

"And you let a beautiful girl like her slip through your fingers?" Hudson shook his head in a disappointed manner. "That's a damn shame."

Tripp couldn't disagree. "When we met, I was in the middle of my residency training in pediatric surgery and my schedule was insane," he said, remembering the long days and even longer nights of studying, rotations, and grabbing sleep at the hospital whenever he could. "There was no room in my life for a committed relationship with any woman. And because I knew Skye wanted to get married and have kids, ending things with her was the right thing to do because I couldn't make that promise." It had also been one of the most painful things, because despite his no-strings-attached rule, he'd fallen in love with her.

Hudson nodded in understanding. "Been there, done that."

"A few months after breaking things off, I saw on social media that she met a guy named Jack and within a year they were married," he said, absently wiping away the condensation on his bourbon glass with his fingers, while trying not to remember the spear of jealousy he'd experienced at the time. "I'm sure that kids followed soon after."

"You unfriended her?" he asked, sounding surprised that he didn't know for sure.

"No. I probably should have," he said with a small laugh, because he'd been way too obsessive about following a woman he'd broken up with. "She deactivated all her social media accounts right after she got married." Which had been odd to him, knowing Skye was social and enjoyed her friends.

It had been hell for him, no longer having any contact or awareness about Skye and her activities, but also a relief. He no longer had to watch her life play out with another man.

Hudson sat back in his seat. "Look, why don't you at least go over there and say hi. There's nothing wrong with saying hello to an old friend. And maybe there's a reason why she's not wearing a ring."

His friend had a point. If he discovered Skye was happy, he'd say hi and walk away. No way would he want to interfere with her life, even if his gut churned at the thought of finding out she was still married. However, if that ringless finger indicated that she was single again, well, as far as he was concerned, all bets were off.

"Better decide quick," Hudson said, nodding toward the bar. "She and her friend are paying their tab and getting ready to leave. Who knows if you'll run into her again."

Without any more hesitation, Tripp stood and

headed toward the bar, his heart hammering wildly in his chest, from the sheer anticipation of being in Skye's space again. He caught up to her just as she slid off her stool and turned, promptly bumping into him. She sucked in a startled breath, and when she faltered on her heels, he reached out and grabbed her arms to steady her.

He registered two things immediately. The way her entire body tensed when he touched her, and the fact that she stared at his chest, as though she feared making eye contact with whoever she'd walked into.

"I'm so sorry," she blurted out in a rush, still staring straight ahead. "I wasn't paying attention—"

"Skye," he said, the word a subtle order for her to *look* up. Saying her name meant he knew her and was meant to shake her out of wherever her mind had gone.

It worked. Even in heels, she'd always been petite, and she finally tipped her head back, her cornflower blue eyes meeting his . . . and Jesus, she was still so damn beautiful she took his breath away.

He smiled at the shock playing across her face as she recognized him, and he gently brushed his thumbs against her bare arms, as much to ease the tension from her body as it was to feel her soft, silky skin beneath his fingers.

She shivered in response and relaxed slightly, and he didn't miss the awareness—and something else he couldn't quite define—that flickered in her gaze as she tried to regain her equilibrium.

Seemingly flustered, she greeted him with a nervous, and shrill, "Hi!"

He chuckled, seeing a small glimpse of the adorably awkward Skye she'd been when they'd first met, even if there was something more reserved about her now.

"Hi yourself," he replied, and now that she was steady on her feet, he reluctantly released her arms. "It's good to see you."

She cleared her throat, as if making sure that the squeak in her voice was gone. "You, too," she replied, more composed now, even if she was staring at him in wide-eyed awe.

He slid his gaze past Skye for a moment to address her friend, Lauren, who he recognized from the massive Dare/Kingston circle of family and friends they were both a part of since his brother, Beck, had married Chloe Kingston. Hell, this bar, The Back Door, was owned and operated by Zach Dare.

Yeah, figuring out the whole family and friends dynamic, and how they were connected to either the Dares or the Kingstons or both, could make a person's head spin. Case in point, Lauren hanging out with Skye as if they were old friends. How did they even know one another?

It didn't escape his notice that Lauren was watching the interaction between himself and Skye with undisguised interest. "Hi, Lauren," he greeted her. "Nice to see you."

She adjusted the strap of her purse over her shoulder and smiled. "Same. You know Skye?"

He nodded. "We met in Boston while I was in med school," he said, keeping the explanation short and simple.

"Wow, small world," Lauren said with a laugh. "By the way, I just saw that you're one of the bachelors up for auction at next week's Future Fast Track charity event."

He grimaced at the reminder. "Yeah. Chloe managed to twist my arm, and Drew's," he said of his other single brother, then returned his attention back to Skye, the only woman in the bar he wanted to focus on. "I have to say I'm shocked to see you in New York City. Are you here with your husband?"

Yeah, he went there. Might as well address his biggest question and get it out in the open, because her answer would decide what he did next.

"No, I'm divorced," she said, and there was no sadness in her voice, but rather a steely conviction that surprised him. "I live in New York now and work with Lauren at the Meridian Hotel."

Perfect. "Would you like to stay? Have a drink and catch up?" he asked. Clearly, a lot had changed in the past five years.

"I . . . umm."

She hesitated, contemplating his invitation as she bit her bottom lip—another one of those quirks he loved. Waiting for her answer was one of those defining moments, because if Skye turned him down, then she'd well and truly moved on.

Finally, she smiled… and nodded. "Yeah, I'd like that."

Relief surged through him. That she'd agreed to have a drink with him made Tripp hope that there was something still there between them, despite *everything* in the past. Time would tell, and he was just happy to spend the next few hours in her presence.

"Well, I'm going to grab an Uber and head out so you two can reconnect." Lauren gave Skye a hug. "I'll see you in the office on Monday."

Skye said goodbye, then glanced around the bar area. "The place is packed. Looks like all the seats are taken." A couple had even slid into the chairs behind Skye where they'd been sitting.

Tripp glanced across the room, catching sight of Hudson, who was still at their table, watching his interaction with Skye. "I have a table in the back corner, where it's quieter. My friend who I came here with is still sitting there."

He automatically placed his hand at the small of Skye's back to guide her in that direction. When he touched her, she tensed again, more subtly this time but it was obvious to him anyway. Then she immediately eased out a breath and her muscles relaxed, as if she'd recognized he was someone who wouldn't hurt her.

He frowned at the thought. Her reaction disturbed him. Back when they'd dated, she'd been a touchy-feely kind of girl, uninhibited and outgoing, and she openly expressed physical affection. She'd accepted his touches just as easily.

Now, she seemed more cautious and guarded. Granted, it had been years since they'd seen one another, but something had subdued that carefree spirit of hers. And he didn't like it one bit.

Hudson stood as they reached the table and pulled out a chair for Skye while smirking at Tripp. "Seems as though I was right, wasn't I?" he said, obviously referring to his guess that Skye was no longer married.

"Seems like you have a knack for being right about a lot of things," Tripp said in a wry tone.

Hudson grinned. "That's because I'm older and wiser than you."

"You'll get no argument from me, *old timer*," he shot back.

Skye, now looking amused at their easy-going ribbing, glanced back at Hudson. "What were you right about?"

"You being a stunningly beautiful woman," his friend said without missing a beat, making Skye blush at his compliment before he met Tripp's gaze. "Aren't you going to introduce me to your guest?"

"Hudson, this is Skye," Tripp said, as she settled into the vacant chair his friend had pulled out for her. "Skye, this is my business partner."

That engaged her interest, and her eyes widened in curiosity. "What kind of business?"

So, she clearly hadn't stalked his social media like he had hers. "We own a family practice together, along with another doctor, Brett," Tripp explained. "I'm in pediatrics. Hudson specializes in internal medicine, and Brett is an obstetrician."

"That's impressive," she replied, and extended her hand toward Hudson. "It's nice to meet you."

His friend took her hand, holding it in his for longer than was necessary, in Tripp's opinion. "The pleasure is all mine," Hudson said in that smooth, suave way of his.

Tripp rolled his eyes, doing his best to conceal his annoyance. Or was it pure possessiveness that was making him feel irritated with Hudson's flirtations? "Don't you need to be somewhere?" Tripp asked, doing his best not to grind his teeth and chip a molar.

"Not that I can recall," Hudson drawled. He finally released Skye's hand, the gleam in his eyes telling Tripp his friend had been goading him on purpose and enjoying Tripp's territorial reaction.

For an aggravating moment Tripp thought Hudson was going to stay and be the annoying third wheel.

"But I can take a hint," he said and Tripp relaxed. "I wouldn't want to share Skye with anyone, either." Hudson gave her a charming wink. "Have a good evening, and I hope I have the pleasure of seeing you again soon."

Skye smiled at him. "Thank you."

"Have a good weekend, Tripp," Hudson said, then headed out for the evening.

When he was gone, Skye glanced at Tripp, her eyes sparkling with mirth. "He's quite the charmer."

Tripp groaned as he slid into the chair right next to

Skye's. "Don't *ever* tell him that. It'll go to his head and he already has an inflated ego." He was teasing, of course. Tripp had a great relationship with both Hudson and Brett, who were like brothers to him. Hence, how easy it was to push each other's buttons.

He'd deliberately chosen the seat right beside Skye's, instead of across from her, so they could talk without yelling over the noise in the bar. But sitting side by side, he realized it put them in very close proximity, and the onslaught of memories was almost instantaneous.

When he inhaled, he caught her light floral scent that made him want to bury his nose against her neck and breathe her in. Their thighs brushed, resulting in an arousal that was thankfully hidden by the table above his lap. And he could clearly see her beautiful face, her delicate features, and those lush, pink lips that made him remember hot, intimate moments that caused his stomach to also heat with anticipation. Then there was her glorious mane of blonde hair that beckoned for him to tangle his fingers through the silken strands, and pull just hard enough to make her gasp and moan.

The blouse she wore was loose, but there was no mistaking the soft fullness of her breasts beneath, or the modest peek of lace he glimpsed at her cleavage. Everything about Skye was sexy, in an understated way. Elegant and classy . . . until he had her in the bedroom, where she used to drop every inhibition and enjoyed all the dirty, filthy ways he seduced her.

He lifted his gaze back to hers, the mutual awareness in her eyes startling him. As did the way her
tongue absently licked across her bottom lip and a
faint pink tinge rose in her cheeks.

Then again, maybe her reaction to him ogling her
shouldn't surprise him. From the moment they'd first
met, they'd been physically in tune to each other's
needs, their thoughts, feelings, and lust also aligned.
All it took was one look, one touch, one whispered
word, and they were desperate to find a secluded place
to tear each other's clothes off. Clearly, their mutual
desire hadn't changed.

He had the insane urge to slide his hand around
the nape of her neck, lean in and kiss her parted lips,
just to confirm that attraction. But the arrival of the
bar waitress kept him from following through on the
impulse. Which was probably for the best. Just because they were still attracted to each other, and Skye
was single and available, didn't mean she'd welcome a
kiss.

"Can I get you two something to drink or eat?" the
friendly young woman asked as she placed fresh
cocktail napkins on the table.

Skye cleared her throat and shifted her gaze to the
waitress. "I'll have a Pellegrino if you have it, please."

"I'll have the same," Tripp said.

As soon as the girl was gone and they were alone
again, Skye returned her attention to him, a small
frown marring her brows. "So, back at the bar when I
ran into you, you asked if I was in New York with my

husband. How did you know I was once married?"

He saw no reason to lie, or even fudge the truth. "I saw it on social media, before you deactivated your accounts. I still followed you even after things ended between us."

Her eyes widened in surprise. He didn't blame her, considering he'd been the one to break things off with her. "*Why?*"

"Because . . . I cared about you," he said, sharing more honesty. "Just because I couldn't give you what you wanted and needed at that time in your life, it didn't mean it wasn't a difficult decision for me to make."

No, it had been an excruciating one, but at the time he'd been nowhere near ready to settle down, get married, and start a family, and he'd told himself she deserved to find that with another man, and thought she had.

Her chin lifted a fraction, and he caught the quick flash of pain in her eyes before she blinked away the emotion. "Didn't seem like a difficult choice at the time."

Those words felt like a stab in the heart. "The last thing I ever wanted to do was hurt you—"

"It's okay," she said with an indifferent shrug he saw right through. "It's water under the bridge, as they say. People break up all the time."

Despite her dismissive tone, there was no doubt in his mind that she was trying to hide the fact that he'd hurt her, badly. That even over five years later, their feelings still lingered.

Their drinks arrived and he was grateful for the chance to regroup and find a topic that would steer the conversation away from the painful part of their past. The waitress placed their bottles of Pellegrino and two glasses of ice on the table, then moved on to another customer. When she was gone, he poured the water over the ice, and Skye did the same.

"Have you been divorced long?" he asked in a casual voice, wanting to know if the emotional impact of her marriage ending was still fresh and raw.

She exhaled a deep breath. "Let's see," she said, her tone sarcastic. "I was married for two years, and legally separated for a year and a half since I couldn't get my ex-husband, Jack, to sign the divorce papers because he had delusions of us reconciling. Thankfully, I've been officially divorced for almost a year."

There was no mistaking the bitterness in her voice, and it piqued his curiosity. "Do you mind me asking what happened?"

Staring at her glass of sparkling water, she hesitated, long enough that he wondered if he'd struck a nerve.

"If you'd rather not talk about it, I understand," he quickly amended.

She shook her head, and glanced back at him, her expressive eyes pained once again, but this time Tripp wasn't the reason.

"It was a complicated relationship, and something I don't want to rehash. Let's just say there were a lot of irreconcilable differences that ended our marriage."

The answer was pat and superficial, and he didn't push her to share more. But there wasn't much he could do about the protective feeling rising inside of him as he recalled her stiffening at the slightest touch. Clearly, the marriage had been a turbulent one, and he couldn't help but wonder if that's why she was so guarded and wary now.

"Are there kids involved?" he asked instead. Another thing he'd often wondered about.

She released a harsh laugh. "No, thank God."

Her reply was blunt and filled with anger, and a part of his heart broke for her. For the girl she'd been. All the things she'd wanted and hoped for hadn't come to fruition and she'd deserved to have it all.

He reached out and placed his hand over hers, her skin smooth and warm beneath his palm. "I'm sorry," he said softly, and meant it.

To his surprise and relief she didn't pull away from his touch. "About?"

"The fact that it didn't work out."

"Me, too." She gave him a sad smile. "I only wanted to get married once."

Not wanting to push his luck, he removed his hand from hers. "You can get married again."

She let out a huff. "After everything I went through . . ." She didn't elaborate on what those things were, just shook her head. "I'm not sure I want to get married again."

That statement was huge. And shocking. What the

hell had caused her to be so cynical and jaded?

He didn't push, not when it was something she obviously didn't want to revisit or discuss. And for now, that was okay with him. They were reconnecting, getting to know one another again, and he didn't want to pressure her for answers she wasn't ready to share. He just hoped she opened up to him in time.

Yes, as crazy at it seemed, he was already thinking into the future. Now that he'd run into Skye again, he didn't plan to let her slip through his fingers so easily this time. Over five years ago he'd realized too late that she was *the one*, and now he'd been given a second chance to see if they could rebuild what they'd once had, because the feelings stirring in his chest told him he'd never, ever, completely gotten over her.

He took a drink of his water and steered clear of anything having to do with her ex. "So, what brought you to New York of all places?" he asked.

"I needed a change," she said with a shrug. "And my brother, Spencer, offered to let me stay at his place while I looked for a job and figured out what I was going to do."

Though Tripp knew she had two older brothers, he'd never met her family because he'd always maintained that their relationship was purely friends with benefits, something he regretted now. But he was glad she had a sibling in the city to look after her.

They spent the next hour keeping the conversation casual as they got reacquainted and caught up on each other's lives. She told him about working at the

Meridian hotel, which is where she'd met Lauren, who was now a good friend, and how she had her own apartment in Brooklyn. He explained the connection between her boss, Jade Dare, and his brother's wife— and Tripp's sister-in-law—Chloe Kingston, who Skye had met a few times already because of how the two families overlapped so much.

He'd already told her about being a pediatrician in business with Hudson and Brett, but he shared a few more details about his career.

"I'm really proud of you and what you've accomplished," she said, and he couldn't deny the compliment warmed him. "You sacrificed a lot to achieve your goals, and it's very impressive."

He didn't like that he'd sacrificed *her* in the process, but hindsight was a bitch.

The bar waitress came around again and cleared their empty bottles and glasses from the table. He and Skye declined another drink, and since the place was getting crowded and overly loud, he gave the waitress his credit card for the bill but he was reluctant to let Skye out of his sight again.

Elbow braced on the table, Skye propped her chin in her palm and smiled, seemingly more relaxed with him than she'd been all evening. "So, you've been quite vague about your own love life," she pointed out, a glimmer of curiosity in her eyes. "Considering Lauren spilled the beans about you being one of the guys in the charity auction at the Future Fast Track fundraiser next weekend, I take it you're still a bachelor?"

"Yes, still single." But not for a lack of trying to move on from Skye, once med school and his residency were behind him and he'd finally felt settled and in a place where he could devote more time to a relationship.

He'd dated Julia, a pharmaceutical rep he'd met at a conference, for almost a year and a half. They'd had fun together, and had been a good match, even if he had compared her too much to Skye and knew she was the polar opposite of the woman he couldn't forget. Still, knowing he wanted a wife and kids, he'd thought maybe they could build a future together. But when he'd made the suggestion, she'd informed him that she was a career woman first and had no desire to get married and have a family. Then, she'd ended things, stating she didn't want to lead him on . . .

How fucking ironic was that?

Tripp winced at the memory, but he could easily look back and admit that Julia had done him a favor by breaking things off. Otherwise he would have been settling with Julia, and that wouldn't have been fair. To either of them. They hadn't shared a grand passion nor had she been the love of his life, but their relationship had been comfortable, easy, and convenient.

But just like Skye had kept a few secrets from him, Tripp wasn't ready to divulge that relationship, either. Not when it would force him to admit his own failings out loud. They weren't at that point yet.

"Are you dating anyone now?" Skye asked, drawing his attention back to her, and those big blue eyes he could easily get lost in.

He shook his head. "No."

She arched a brow, her demeanor playful. "No time, or you just like playing the field?"

The waitress dropped off the check and his credit card, and Tripp signed the receipt before meeting Skye's gaze again.

"How about I haven't met a woman I've wanted to go out with more than a few times." That was certainly the truth after his break up with Julia nine months ago. "What about you?" he said, putting the focus back on her. "Are you back to dating, at least?"

An incredulous laugh escaped her. "No. I'm not interested in dating. I have a job that I love, and I'm enjoying being on my own. I feel like I'm finally happy again, and settled, and the last thing I need is a man in my life to make me feel whole and complete."

That response felt like a punch in his gut, but he decided to spin her reply in a different direction. "So, you've decided to become a nun then?" he teased, blatantly bringing up the topic of sex.

"I didn't say that." She was grinning at him, but she also paused a moment, as if she wanted to be careful about what she said next. "Would it be nice to have an orgasm with something other than my vibrator? Of course," she said, not shy about admitting she had desires before her expression turned more serious. "But having a man in my life isn't a necessity. And honestly . . . I'm not the same girl I was when we were dating."

Fanciful. Optimistic. A hopeful romantic. There was no denying that part of her personality had changed, because he could see it for himself. She'd taken a chance on a dream with a man she thought she could build a life with, and she'd lost.

The heartache in her eyes wrecked him, and before he could stop himself he reached out and gently smoothed a silky strand of hair from her cheek. "I wouldn't expect you to be the same girl."

She tipped her head toward him just slightly, as if leaning into the warmth of his touch on her face. "The truth is . . . getting involved with any man again scares the crap out of me," she admitted in a soft voice. "I don't trust easily anymore."

What had that asshole done to her? The rage Tripp felt toward her ex that was bubbling beneath the surface was real, and he had to forcibly push that anger aside because there was no one to unleash it on.

As for his sweet Skye, he desperately wanted to erase all that pain and heartbreak. So, he put his hand on the table in front of her, his palm up, his gaze holding hers steadily.

"Do you trust *me*?" he asked. It was a daring question, and a huge risk, one he knew might come with an answer he didn't like, considering how *he'd* hurt her.

She stared at him for a long moment, then a slow, gradual smile touched her lips as she slid her soft palm along his. "Yes, I trust you," she whispered.

He felt the breath leave his lungs, because his

greatest fear was that he'd contributed to her apprehension about men. He wasn't sure what, exactly, they were talking about anymore—sex? Something more?—but it didn't matter. He wasn't willing to part ways with her yet and he hoped she felt the same.

He wove their fingers intimately together, and she let him. "Would you like to go back to my place where it's quiet and we can be alone?" Realizing how that sounded, and not wanting her to think his invitation came with any strings attached—even though he'd love nothing more than to feel her beneath him again—he added, "We can have a drink and just talk and relax—"

"Yes, I'd like that," she said before he could finish.

Relief poured through him. That was all Tripp needed to hear, and he didn't waste any more time getting them out of there.

Chapter Three

THE UBER RIDE to Tripp's place was quiet, but in a way that reminded Skye of how effortless and uncomplicated it was to be with him. The connection between them was still strong, and neither felt the need to fill the silence with idle chit chat. In fact, the lull in conversation was so comfortable that she had to resist the urge to snuggle up against him in the back seat and lay her head on his shoulder, just like old times.

He was still holding her hand—he'd only let go once when she'd slid into the vehicle—and she couldn't deny that she felt safe and secure with him. She'd meant what she'd said when she'd told Tripp that she trusted him. Their past was painful and messy, but he'd always been honest and he'd never intentionally hurt her, which was more than she could say about her ex-husband.

Agreeing to accompany Tripp back to his place had been a surprisingly easy choice, and she'd given her answer knowing where things would most likely lead . . . right into his bed. She'd witnessed the hunger in his eyes when he looked at her at the bar, and that heated lust made her own body come alive. And while she knew he truly had no expectations once they entered his apartment, she'd already made the decision to indulge in her own desire for him.

Seeing Tripp again, and spending time with him, made her ache for the exquisite satisfaction she knew this man could give her. And if she were honest with herself, she'd missed him so much. She'd relied on her battery operated boyfriend to take care of her needs for years now, and she'd be lying if she said she didn't crave physical contact and intimacy. After everything she'd endured in her marriage, tonight she desperately wanted to feel desirable again, and Tripp was the only man she trusted to take those liberties with her body.

He wasn't a random stranger. He was familiar and safe, and she knew exactly what to expect with him. Great orgasms and a night filled with sinful pleasures. And, he knew what she enjoyed in the bedroom—that edge of male dominance that was always tempered in a way that never crossed the line. Unlike her ex. Tripp's touch—no matter how assertive he might have been in the bedroom—had never made her feel afraid or uncomfortable.

She was going into this situation with a clear head and the choice being hers. She was far from wanting a long term commitment from any man. This was all about physical pleasure, for them both. No strings attached—a scenario that Tripp was plenty familiar with.

They arrived at his residential building—an impressively upscale complex located in downtown Manhattan—and with his hand still clasped in hers, he walked her through the lobby to the elevator. Once inside the lift, she could practically feel the sexual tension vibrating between them, though Tripp did nothing more than hit the button for his floor and remain a complete gentleman, much to her disappointment.

The entire ride up, all she could think about was the many times they'd ridden the elevator to his tiny studio back in Boston, both of them unable to keep their hands and mouths off each other the entire way. By the time they reached his apartment, they'd been wild and desperate to fuck against the nearest surface. That same eager anticipation swirled through her now, and by the time they entered his place and he closed the door behind them, she was ready to take what she wanted.

She stopped just inside the living room area, and so did he, finally releasing her hand. Tripp glanced at her, and they stared at one another, his head tipped slightly to the side. No words were spoken, but his dark, sexy gaze glimmered with silent questions she was prepared to answer by making the first move.

For the first time in years, she felt daring and sensual, and she embraced the bold woman emerging from her cocoon. Tossing her purse onto the nearby sofa, she stepped toward Tripp and smoothed her hands up over his chest. He wore a white dress shirt, but the heat of his skin and hard muscles beneath made her body clench with need.

His breathing escalated as he watched her through hooded eyes, clearly waiting to see what she intended as she continued to slide her hands up around his neck, then stood on the tips of her high heels so that her mouth *finally* brushed across his—soft and seductive and enticing. She touched her tongue to his bottom lip, and was rewarded with a low, guttural groan from him that sent a thrill through her.

It was all the invitation he seemed to need as he gripped her hips. His fingers dug into her curves and held on, guiding her backwards until he had her pinned against the nearest wall. The length of his strong, hard body pressed intimately to hers, reacquainting her with the size and length of his cock as that solid ridge of flesh dug into her stomach—also reminding her how much bigger and taller he was than her. Unlike Jack, his height and strength made her feel safe and protected, not threatened.

Once Tripp had her where he wanted her, he framed her face in his hands, and like a man starved for a taste, he dipped his head for a kiss and consumed her, eliciting a soft, helpless whimper from her throat. He stole the sound from her lips, drinking from her deeply, hungrily, as if he were trying to make up for all the lost years between them. He slid his tongue against hers, exploring her, ravishing her, and she twined her fingers in his hair and let him do what he did best when it came to sex.

Take control.

The hot kiss went on for what seemed an impossibly long time before Tripp slowed it down, his lips softly nuzzling hers as they shared deep, gasping breaths. Her entire body was unbearably aroused, from her tight, sensitive nipples, to the heat swirling in her belly, to how her panties were soaked to the point of being ruined.

He finally lifted his mouth from hers, his touch on her face gentling, which contradicted the fierce, possessive gleam in his eyes. She licked her bottom lip and shivered at that intense look, and a low, warning growl rumbled in his chest.

"You're making it very hard for me to be a gentleman," he said huskily.

She deliberately moved her hips against his, tempting and teasing him. "I don't want a drink. I don't want to talk and relax," she said, reiterating the words he'd used earlier at the bar. "And I certainly don't want you to be a gentleman tonight."

A slow, sinful smile tipped up the corners of his mouth as he stroked his fingers along her cheek. "Then what do you want, baby girl?"

That sweet name he'd used to call her made Skye melt inside and added more fuel to the desire already overwhelming her. "You," she whispered, staring directly into his eyes. "Tonight, I want *you*."

He arched a brow, a devilish light in his eyes. "You're going to have to be more specific than that."

She knew how to play these sexy, dirty games with Tripp, since he'd been the one who'd taught her to vocalize her needs. It had been a long time since she'd been able to do that, and knowing how much her bold words turned him on, she didn't hold back. "I want you to fuck me."

"Such a dirty girl," he murmured, approval in his tone. "How about this instead . . . I'm going to make you beg for it first."

"You can certainly try," she said, challenging him.

He touched his fingers beneath her chin, and tipped her head back further, staring down at her. "I was wondering where my feisty, uninhibited girl was," he murmured. "Glad to see she's still there."

She didn't doubt he'd noticed how reserved and guarded she'd been earlier in the bar, and there were certain aspects of her recent past that *still* kept her emotionally cautious. But sexually, there was no reason for her to hold back because with Tripp, she didn't have to worry about saying or doing the wrong thing, or triggering a violent temper.

Intending to give him more of her bold, assertive side, she lowered her hands to the waistband of his slacks, but before she could unbuckle his slim black belt he caught her wrists and stopped her.

"Not so fast," he said with a shake of his head. "Put your hands flat against the wall at your sides and keep them there until I say you can move them."

She followed through with his request, and when he was satisfied that she'd complied he began slowly unbuttoning the front of her blouse, the warm tips of his fingers grazing across her skin. Once the top was completely unfastened, he pulled the hem from the waistband of her jeans, then shoved it down her arms and let it drop to the floor. Instead of removing her bra like she expected him to, he pushed both straps off her shoulders, then peeled the lace cups down, until her full breasts were exposed to his gaze. He left her like that, indecently half-dressed and dying for his illicit touch.

"Fuck, you're beautiful," he murmured huskily, staring down at her chest as he ran his fingers over her stiff nipples, before giving them a pinch that made her gasp and arch her back toward his hand in a silent plea for more.

He smiled knowingly, then dipped his head down, skimming his warm, damp lips, and his tongue, along the side of her neck. A shiver wracked her body, and she had to resist the urge to grab his hair and push his mouth down to her aching nipples. Instead, she kept her hands in place and endured the torment of him licking her skin and slowly kissing his way down to her collarbone.

A whimper of need escaped her before she could stop the sound, and he gave her a little love bite along her bare shoulder, making her knees threaten to buckle.

"Ready to beg yet?" he asked against her ear, sounding way too arrogant about his ability to seduce her, as he should since she was nearly there.

"Not even close," she lied breathlessly.

She felt him smirk against her skin. "Hmm . . .

then let me try a little harder."

He kissed his way down to the swell of her cleavage, then a bit lower. His lips surrounded one peak and sucked it deeply into his mouth, while he cupped the opposite breast, using his fingers to pinch and tweak the nipple. The velvet slide of his tongue swirling around the sensitive tip, along with the graze of his teeth, had her panting for breath and nearly shaking with need.

"Still no pretty pleas falling from your lips?" he murmured, his tone laced with amusement.

Not trusting herself to speak, she shook her head, determined to hold out, if only to extend this decadent pleasure and see what he did next.

He straightened, releasing her breasts and nipple, and gave her a wicked grin. "Looks like I'm going to have to get creative."

He turned her around so that she was facing the wall, her bare breasts pressed against the cool surface, and placed her hands flat beside her head, his no touching rule still in place. He reached around and unfastened her pants and lowered her zipper, then shamelessly pushed his hand inside her underwear. The second his fingers slid between her legs and discovered how aroused she was, he released a low, gratified groan.

He pressed his chest to her back, anchoring her there with the strength and heat of his body. "I think you're lying," he said, putting his mouth near her ear. "You're absolutely soaked."

He continued to stroke her slick pussy, alternating with deeper caresses and an occasional tug of her clit that drove her mad. Her hips started to move back and forth instinctively as she tried to fuck herself on his fingers and attempted to chase the orgasm he held just out of her reach. His other hand played with her breasts, and the solid length of his dick rubbed up against her ass every time she gyrated against him.

The whole situation was so dirty and illicit, and everything she needed. A safe space to let him take control of her body and pleasure, and her being able to let go and just *feel*.

Every time she tipped close to the edge of release, he slowed things down, and she couldn't hold back the frustrated sob that escaped her throat.

"You want to come, baby girl?" he asked, his fingers dancing across her clit once again in a light, teasing rhythm—not nearly enough pressure to get her off.

She made an inarticulate sound and nodded frantically, grinding against his hand in response.

"I want to hear you say the words," he demanded.

"Please," she gasped. "Please make me come."

"Good girl," he murmured, burying his face into the hair cascading along the side of her neck while his fingers gave her what she so desperately needed. "I can't wait to get my mouth on this pussy and lick every inch of you. I already know you taste like fucking candy, but right now, I want you to come all over my hand."

She did exactly as he ordered, her orgasm slamming into her so hard her body jerked against his and she felt her legs give out on her. The hand at her breast immediately moved lower, his arm banding around her waist to hold her up as she sobbed and shook and flew apart in the most glorious, euphoric way.

When the blissful fog finally cleared from her mind and she could think and breathe right again, she rested her head against the wall and sighed. "That was . . . so good, but not nearly enough."

Still pressed up against her from behind, Tripp chuckled, the deep, dirty sound vibrating against her back. "Greedy girl. Now that your first orgasm is out of the way, ask me nicely for what you really want."

She smiled, loving how easy it was to play this game with him, to ask for what she wanted, knowing he'd oblige. "Fuck me, Tripp, *please*."

"Oh, I plan to," he said, and she gasped as he effortlessly swept her into his arms and started carrying her through the living room and down a hallway. "All night long. Or at least until you beg me to stop."

She laughed at his arrogance and wound her arms around his neck, already anticipating one of the best nights of her life.

✧   ✧   ✧

TRIPP TOOK SKYE to his bedroom and placed her on his bed, right where she belonged. He didn't waste any time getting her completely naked, stripping off her bra and removing her shoes, jeans, and panties, then let her recline back on the mattress while he rid himself of his own clothes.

Her skin was flushed, not out of modesty, but from the orgasm he'd just given her, and her skin pinkened even more as she watched through half-mast eyes as he quickly shed his own garments, until he was just as bare. She bit her bottom lip, her gaze traveling from his face, down his chest and abs, to his groin. She stared at his thick, erect cock as she squirmed on the mattress impatiently. He retrieved a condom from the nightstand and sheathed his dick.

How many times had he imagined this scenario—Skye spread out on his bed, her glorious silky hair sweeping across his pillow and that come hither look in her eyes inviting him to bury his cock deep inside her body. It was a reoccurring fantasy he visited whenever he needed an image to jack off to, but tonight, she was his reality and he planned to enjoy every single second with her.

He walked to the foot of the bed, keeping his eyes on her. "Spread your legs nice and wide for me."

His blood heated in his veins when she parted those smooth thighs without an ounce of hesitation and gave him a perfect view of her pussy, pink and swollen and glistening with her arousal. A soft, coy smile curved her lips, and he was glad to see that she had no reservations when it came to her desires and what she wanted. That much, at least, hadn't changed between them.

He moved onto the bed and between her splayed legs, pushing them further apart as he settled face first in between. Smoothing his palms along the outside of her thighs and up to her hips, he held her in place as he covered her with his mouth, sliding his tongue between the lips of her sex before thrusting deep and licking into her.

She moaned, long and loud, and twisted her fingers in his hair as he inhaled the peachy scent of her skin mixed with the womanly musk of her aroused body that went straight to his throbbing dick. Knowing exactly what she liked, and exactly what she needed to orgasm a second time, he sucked her clit, swirling and flicking his tongue against that firm nub.

She arched toward his hungry mouth as he continued feasting and licking and sucking, driving her higher and higher until there was nothing left for her to do but fall over the edge with a soft cry of pleasure. Her body undulated, the epitome of pure, sensual, uninhibited woman as she rode out her release.

When the intensity ebbed, he sat up on his knees. Skye was still quivering, her gasps slowly turning into indulgent sighs of satisfaction as she lay there in a limp, boneless heap. Her legs were open, the tender skin on the inside of her thighs marked and a bit chafed by his evening stubble. She looked utterly wanton, and he had the overwhelming need to be inside her.

To claim her. To own her. To make her his again.

He moved over her, catching her lips in a hungry kiss as he pulled one of her legs up around his hip and opened her even wider for his ultimate possession. The wet heat of her pussy anointed the head of his cock as it sank between her folds and then pressed into her tight, slick core.

She gasped against his lips and he groaned, feeling her slender body stretching to reacquaint itself with his size as he pushed into her, inch by inch, until he was buried to the hilt and right where he needed to be.

He lifted his head so that he could stare down at her face, so he could look into her eyes as he wrung even more pleasure from her body while he fucked her.

"So fucking perfect," he said, his voice gruff as he started to move inside her. Slow and steady at first, but when she wrapped her legs around his waist and angled her hips to take him even deeper, the last remnants of his control unraveled.

His next thrust was a little harder. The one after that harder still. Each lunge and grind against her sex dragged an uninhibited groan from her throat that only spurred him on.

"More," she whispered raggedly, raking her nails down his back as she tossed her head back against the pillow.

He wrapped his fingers in her hair to hold on as he gave her everything he had, driving faster, pumping infinitely deeper, the moment between them so elemental and primal. Instinct took over as they rocked against one another, completely in sync. Their movements turned frantic as the tension increased until finally, she cried out his name and her body shuddered beneath his, the clenching of her core around his cock more than enough to bring him right along with her.

Everything about Skye intoxicated him, and driven by the need to utterly possess her, he sealed his lips against hers and kissed her hungrily while waves of heat pulsed through him, followed by a long, intense orgasm that left him wasted.

He stayed on top of her for a long time, still inside her, both of their breathing ragged and his heart pounding crazily against hers. And not just from the exertion of rigorous sex.

No, this feeling was much more fundamental and intrinsic ... because now that he'd had Skye again, now that she was back in his life, he was going to do everything in his power to make sure she stayed there.

Chapter Four

SKYE WOKE UP slowly the following morning, stretching in an unfamiliar bed and momentarily disoriented by her surroundings and the savory scents and muted sounds coming from another area of the apartment. Not *her* apartment, but Tripp's, she quickly remembered as memories of last night came rushing into her mind. Those erotic recollections, combined with the way the muscles in her thighs ached, and how sated she felt, brought a smile to her face.

In a city as large as New York, Skye still couldn't believe that she'd run into Tripp, but in the aftermath of many pleasurable orgasms she was glad she had—though it wasn't just about the sex, but that connection she still felt with him. Being comfortable around Tripp and the fact that she trusted him implicitly, as a friend and a lover, was a nice feeling after being so cautious and reserved around men since her divorce.

It had been much too long since she'd experienced the kind of desire and need that Tripp so effortlessly coaxed out of her, and the entire night with him had been nothing short of amazing.

Sex with Jack, especially once they were married,

had turned into a chore. Anything physical between them had been all about him taking what he wanted, even if it made her uncomfortable, and giving very little in return. He'd treated her like an object, devoid of thought or feeling, reducing her down to little more than a possession. At first, it had been easier to just go through the motions than deal with his snide remarks, his verbal abuse, and the belittling that made her feel flawed and inadequate.

Pleasing Jack, in any aspect of their marriage, had been impossible, and eventually she'd made excuses not to be touched—which hadn't gone over well with him at all. But he'd been a master at gaslighting and emotional manipulation, turning any situation around on her and making her question her perception of reality, until she'd operated at a heightened level of anxiety and was always apologizing for shit she didn't do. He'd accused her of cheating, of being paranoid, and isolated her from friends and family.

He did it all to gain power and control over every aspect of her life, and for a woman who considered herself intelligent and self-aware prior to meeting Jack, she'd somehow fallen into his trap until she'd discovered *his* affair. She'd had irrefutable proof and confronted him, and of course he'd tried to make her feel responsible for the fact that he'd fucked another woman.

This time, she hadn't backed down from their heated argument, or his intimidating stance. That show of defiance had pissed him off even more, and he'd shoved her against the wall and punched her in the face so hard she'd seen stars. It had been the first time he'd hit her. The first time anyone had laid a hand on her in violence, and there had been no apology or remorse. But that slug in the face was more than enough to make her *finally* take a hard look at her life, her turbulent two year marriage, and just how shattered and broken she'd become.

That weekend, she'd packed up her things and left—though he hadn't made the separation and ensuing divorce easy on her. No, for a while he'd stalked and harassed her, until she had a restraining order issued against him, then moved to New York to put a safe, physical distance between them, as well.

Skye rolled to her back on the soft bed and exhaled a deep breath, expelling those darks thoughts that had no business being in her head after her unforgettable night with Tripp. He was all she wanted to think about, and as she replayed the evenings provocative festivities in her mind, that awful twist in her stomach dissipated and a genuine smile gradually replaced her somber mood.

More soft clanking sounds from the front of the apartment piqued her interest, as did the alluring scent of coffee and bacon. Breakfast beckoned her grumbling stomach, and she moved off the bed, still completely naked. Seeing the white dress shirt Tripp had worn yesterday draped over a chair in the corner of the room, she put it on, taking a moment to bury her face in the fabric and inhale the heady, masculine scent that clung to the material.

Despite numerous orgasms and the many different ways Tripp had fucked her, arousal pooled low in her belly, as if her body was programmed to respond just to his smell alone. She padded into the bathroom, took care of business, and as she washed her hands she noticed a toothbrush sitting on the vanity, still in its store packaging.

The thoughtful gesture warmed her, and she brushed her teeth then ran her fingers through her hair, doing her best to bring some order to the disheveled mess. She caught sight of a faint discoloration on her neck, a hickey Tripp had obviously given her at some point, and grinned at her reflection. She hadn't had a hickey, well, since the last time he'd marked her with one.

As much as she liked the feeling of him claiming her, she had every intention of keeping her head on straight about last night's hookup. Most importantly, she didn't want to lead Tripp on in any way, because she wasn't looking for anything serious or a committed relationship. Being tied down to a man wasn't a part of her future plans, especially since making the decision to have a baby on her own . . . a process she expected to start in the next few months.

But for now, Tripp Daniels was a great distraction, and one she intended to enjoy until the insemination process began.

✧   ✧   ✧

Tripp placed the last strip of crisp bacon on a plate next to the scrambled eggs he'd also made, just as Skye strolled into the kitchen, looking well and truly fucked with her tousled hair, the glow on her face, and the small hickey he spied on her neck.

He had to curb the ridiculous impulse to beat on his chest like a primal caveman.

She greeted him with an almost shy smile, no surprise considering all the wicked ways he'd defiled her during the course of the night. "Good morning."

Her soft, husky voice was like a shot of lust straight to his dick, as was seeing her in the white dress shirt of his that she'd chosen to wear. Being petite in stature, the hem almost hit her knees and would have been considered modest if it wasn't for the fact that she'd left more than a few buttons undone down the front. Low enough to give him a glimpse of the curves of her supple breasts. Her nipples poked against the front, and he could see the dusky shadows of her areolas through the fabric.

She looked sexy as fuck and he had to resist the urge to bend her over the table and corrupt her even more. He always loved how she'd wear his shirts the morning after a hookup, how the visual would make him think, *I got laid and now it's official and she's mine.* And mostly, how proprietary it made him feel to know she was wrapped up in his scent—yeah, like a damn dog marking their territory. It galled him to think he'd let her go. He'd been such a goddamn fool.

Unable to stop himself, he closed the distance between them, slid an arm around her waist to bring her body flush to his, and pressed his mouth to hers, kissing her good morning. She placed her hands on his bare chest, parted her lips on a tiny, welcoming sigh, and let him deepen the connection. She tasted warm, soft, and minty-sweet.

In time, he lifted his mouth from hers, but didn't let her go. "I would think you'd remember what seeing you in one of my shirts does for me," he said, absently sliding his hand up the back of her thigh beneath the hem, only to encounter her bare, smooth ass. He groaned. "And you're not wearing anything underneath. Jesus, you're killing me." She had to feel the stiff erection digging into her lower stomach through his sweatpants.

She laughed, her expression amused. "I can't believe you can still get hard after how many times we had sex. I'm so sore . . . in a really good way, though."

He smirked down at her. "Want me to kiss it and make it better?"

"God, you're incorrigible." She lightly smacked his chest, then playfully pushed him away. "How about you feed me. I burned a lot of calories trying to keep up with you and I'm hungry."

He chuckled, and even though he was thoroughly enjoying their light-hearted banter, he finally released her so he could serve up their breakfast. "Help yourself to a cup of coffee," he said, nodding toward the Keurig on the counter, along with the mug, creamer, and sugar he'd left out for her.

While she filled her cup, he brought their plates and forks to the table, and retrieved two glasses of orange juice. They sat down, and as she took a few bites of her eggs, then a piece of cantaloupe, her eyes took in his apartment in the morning light.

He'd left the drapes open last night, and now the sun streamed through, brightening up the living room and kitchen area. Out the plate glass windows was a coveted view of the iconic New York City skyline, which for most people, didn't come cheap.

"This is a fantastic place," she said, a bit of awe in her voice. "You must be doing very well for yourself."

"I am," he said, proud of the thriving practice he operated with Brett and Hudson that afforded him many luxuries. "But I also have a brother who is in high end real estate and he owns this building, which makes things much more affordable."

Her mouth literally dropped open in shock. "Wow. That's impressive." She regained her composure and picked up a piece of bacon. "Which brother would that be? You have two, right?"

He nodded. "Yes, and it's Beck, the youngest."

"That would be Chloe Kingston's husband," she said almost absently, then gave him an impish grin. "I'm still trying to keep all the Kingstons and Dares straight in my head. There's so many different people that intersect."

He laughed in agreement. "It can definitely get overwhelming."

"And your other brother?" she asked curiously,

stabbing a slice of cantaloupe with her fork. "What does he do?"

"Drew is a lawyer. Mergers and acquisitions," he explained, realizing that during their previous six months together in Boston, he hadn't shared much about his family, just the basics since they all lived in a different state. "He's the one taking part in the bachelor auction next weekend, too."

For the first time since agreeing to Chloe's request to put himself on the fundraiser block, Tripp experienced a real stab of regret. The last thing he wanted to do was spend time with any woman other than Skye, but he'd made the commitment and he'd follow through. Besides, he told himself that just because someone bid on him for a weekend didn't mean it came with expectations.

But the thought of dating anyone else, even for the sake of charity, sat in his stomach like lead.

"And your parents?" she asked, continuing the stream of casual conversation before taking a drink of her orange juice. "Do they live in the area?"

He finished eating his forkful of eggs before replying. "Yes. They're retired and live in Nassau County."

She smiled at him. "They haven't relocated to Florida, or a warmer climate for retirement?"

He laughed and shook his head. "No. I don't think they'll ever move from the house they're living in."

She tipped her head to the side curiously. "Why not?"

"Remember me telling you about my twin, Whitney?" Mentioning his sister to Skye five years prior had been brief, too, mainly because losing his sibling had been such a deeply personal thing and he'd buried the grief and pain for a very long time.

"Yes," she said softly, her expression filled with compassion. "That she passed away of leukemia when you were sixteen."

The sorrow was definitely still there, now dulled by time. "Well, we all grew up in that house and every year since she passed, I've planted a rose bush in the back yard on the date of her passing. This year will be the twentieth one I'll plant for her. Next month, to be exact."

"Oh, wow, they must look beautiful when they all blossom," she said in awe. "What an amazing thing to do to honor your sister's memory. Now I understand why your parents wouldn't want to move. Something like that would be so hard to leave behind."

"My parents are happy there," he said, setting his fork down on his empty plate. "And now that Beck and Chloe have given them a grandchild, they're not going anywhere. They adore the baby. Chloe and Beck named her Whitney, after my sister."

"I love that," she replied, before finishing off her orange juice. "Thank you for breakfast, by the way."

"The least I can do is feed you," he teased, and wanting his time with her to last even longer, he quickly said, "Want to hang out today? I was supposed to meet my brother at the gym in about an hour, but I can cancel."

"No, don't do that. I really need to go," she replied, toying with the handle of her coffee mug and glancing away in a manner that felt as though she was already trying to put distance between them when he wanted the opposite. "It's Sunday and I have things I need to do today before the work week starts. And this week is going to be extremely busy leading up to the Future Fast Track charity event at the Meridian next weekend."

The fact that she wouldn't meet his gaze was a disconnect between them he didn't like at all. She'd let her guard down last night just enough to enjoy sex with him, but now, those walls seemed to be rising again. He wanted nothing more than to call her out on her retreating back to the reserved woman he'd first bumped into last night, but he refrained.

Tripp already knew being with Skye wasn't a short term thing for him. So, he had to look at the long game, be patient, and give her time to work through whatever shit her ex had put her through. Only then would she trust him with more than just her body. Ultimately, he wanted her heart, and he was willing to do whatever it took to win her, because he already knew she was worth the wait and the effort.

"Okay," he said, standing and grabbing their plates and utensils. "Why don't you get changed and I'll clean up the kitchen."

She gave him a faint smile, but didn't argue as she grabbed her purse from where she'd tossed it on the couch last night and headed back to his bedroom.

He loaded up the dishwasher, and by the time he was done cleaning the counters and stovetop, she reentered the kitchen wearing the same outfit as the previous night. Her face was free of make-up, except for a slight gloss on her lips along with some kind of clip or rubber band that was now holding her hair in a messy bun on top of her head. Still, she looked breathtakingly beautiful.

"I guess I should go," she said, shifting on her heels a bit awkwardly, a direct contradiction to the confident woman who'd been in his bed.

Before she could head out of the kitchen to the front door, he spoke up. "What are we doing here, Skye?" he asked, curious to know where her head was at and what to expect in terms of them. "You and me."

She shrugged, trying to appear nonchalant. "Sex? Fun, no strings attached hookups?"

He arched a brow, hating the way that sounded. "Is that all I am to you?"

Something in her eyes flashed but was gone before he could fully decipher it. "You've never had an issue being friends with benefits before."

Yeah, that direct shot fucking burned, but she was right. That's all he'd offered her in the past. "So that's what we are? Friends having sex?" Because for now, he'd take it over nothing at all.

"Sounds like a perfect arrangement to me," she said, a bit too flippantly. "At least until I get pregnant."

His entire body stiffened, as if he'd heard that proverbial record scratch in his head, where everything came to a screeching halt because he was certain he'd misheard her. "What did you say?"

She cringed, her face flushing pink, as if she couldn't believe she'd spoken the words, either. "That came out sounding *really* bad," she said quickly. "I didn't mean until I get pregnant from having sex with *you.*"

What the ever-loving fuck? "You plan on getting pregnant by someone else?" he asked incredulously.

"Yes." She winced again, now looking embarrassed. "Shit, that sounded worse."

It sure as hell did, and the mere thought of another man impregnating her made him feel nuclear. "Care to explain?" he asked with forced calm.

"Yes, I do." She set her purse on the table and sat in one of the chairs. Her palms absently rubbed along her denim clad thighs as she met his gaze. "Actually, there *is* something you should know. I mean, you'll find out eventually and it's not something I'm keeping secret. I just didn't think we'd need to have this as a morning after conversation."

He could tell she was nervous, but he leaned against the nearest counter, crossed his arms over his chest, and remained quiet, refusing to do or say a thing to deter this discussion until she gave him answers.

"I want to have a baby, on my own," she said on a rush of breath. "I've already looked into it and I plan to get artificially inseminated."

His jaw nearly dropped to the floor in shock. "With some guy's random sperm and a turkey baster?"

She pursed her lips in annoyance. "They don't use a turkey baster, and it's not random. It's actually a specific process to find a sperm donor, and I've spent the past few months researching and looking into possible donors based on what I want genes-wise."

His mind was spinning as he tried to process what she was saying—that she was already planning a future. One that obviously didn't include him, since they'd just ran into each other last night. But the pain in his chest told him that Skye going the sperm donation route was not an option. Not for him.

When it came to Skye, she was his. "You're serious about this?"

"Yes." She lifted her chin. "Things might not have worked out with Jack, but that doesn't mean I can't have the child I've always wanted."

"I'll do it," he blurted out, and there wasn't one part of him that regretted the spontaneous words. If this is what she wanted, he was all in, because the mere thought of a random stranger being her baby's father made his stomach churn.

A small frown formed between her brows. "You'll do what, exactly?" she asked.

"I'll give you my sperm," he said, meaning it. "I'll give you a baby."

She laughed, the sound strained. "I know we made that silly promise about you being my baby daddy back when we were dating, but really, you're off the hook."

He pushed off the counter and joined her at the table. Pulling out the chair next to hers, he sat in the seat facing her, so there was no way for her to hide. He grabbed her hands and held them gently as he stared into her eyes.

"I'm serious, Skye. I'll do it." Because the image of her carrying another man's child, and him losing her before he even had the chance to prove he was still in love with her, ate at his gut like acid.

She sighed. "Tripp . . . as much as I like the idea because I *know* you, giving me a baby could get complicated."

He smiled and brushed his thumbs along the back of her hands. "It doesn't have to be."

She pulled her fingers from his and placed them in her lap. Her lips firmed in a straight line. "After Jack, well, I'm not looking to get married, or even be tied down. Having a child with you would bind us for the rest of our lives, and I'm sure you don't want that responsibility."

He understood why she'd believe that of him but he'd grown up. Changed. He'd lived life without her and understood all he'd lost.

"What if I told you that I do want kids? That at thirty-six and already established in my career, I'm *ready* for them? I'm pushing forty in the next few years, and I don't foresee any future prospects for my wife." On that last point, he lied, knowing he'd scared the shit out of her if he came on too strong.

She was strong in the bedroom but outside of it,

he saw the changes, the skittishness and wariness that her bastard ex-husband had caused. If he flat-out asked her to marry him, and share the whole wife, family, house and future, he knew she'd bolt.

Since she stared at him, lips parted in shock, he continued to press his cause. "If you can be a single mother, why can't I be a single dad? Then your baby, *our baby*, would at least have a father figure in his or her life, forever."

"Tripp—"

"We could co-parent as friends," he interrupted, knowing she was about to shoot him down. Even though he hated the impersonal way his proposition sounded, all he needed was an in. A chance to win her back. "I'll agree to whatever terms you'd like, so long as I'm a part of the kid's life. That's my only stipulations."

She smiled sadly. "See, complicated."

"It doesn't have to be." He sat back in his chair, prepared to give her all the reasons why it could work. "The child would have a mother and a father, you'd know the baby's health history, and our baby would be loved by my family, too. This isn't the dark ages, Skye. Plenty of people choose to have kids out of wedlock and co-parent. It's not an antiquated concept."

She bit her bottom lip, but didn't look convinced.

He tamped down his frustration. "Look, just think about it before you start the insemination process, okay?" he asked in a gentle tone. "I honestly believe that the pros outweigh the cons of you picking some random donor. Can you promise me that you'll at least consider the idea?"

She thought for a long moment, then exhaled a deep breath. "Okay, fine," she said.

He knew she was trying to placate him, but at least he'd planted the idea, and hoped it took root. "And I know you're busy this week, but I'd like to stay in touch, at least by text, if that's okay with you?"

She nodded, and smiled. "Yes, it is."

"I'll see you next week at the fundraiser." God, how was he going to survive seven fucking days without seeing or touching her?

She nodded, and he pulled her into his arms for a warm hug and placed a soft, chaste kiss on her temple before releasing her. Letting her walk out his door was difficult, but he had to give her space and time to mull things over, without pressure or demands.

Because as much as Tripp wanted this with Skye, it was ultimately her decision. No matter how much a *no* would devastate him.

Chapter Five

MORNINGS AT THE medical office usually started the same way, and Monday was no different. Tripp, Hudson and Brett showed up earlier than the front-end staff to review their day's appointments before patients began arriving. The first person to get in always made a pot of coffee—which today was Tripp—and they usually met in the break room to drink their cups of much needed caffeine and shoot the shit before heading to their individual offices to go over patient files before the practice opened.

Brett walked in first, with Hudson following right behind. Brett was in his early forties, which made Tripp the youngest doctor in the practice. The other man dragged his fingers through his sandy blond hair and headed straight for the coffee machine, which had just stopped percolating.

"Hey, Tripp," Brett said, pouring a mug of the steaming brew. "How was your weekend?"

He asked the question just as Tripp took a drink of his coffee, which gave Hudson plenty of opportunity to quickly interject.

"Hopefully you didn't crash and burn with the

lovely Skye, and got laid instead," Hudson said with a smirk.

Tripp frowned at him. "Don't be an asshole."

Hudson filled his own cup, humor dancing in his eyes. "Hmm. Do I detect a defensive tone in your voice? Wait, don't tell me. You're being chivalrous and protecting Skye's honor." Humor turned to a roll of his eyes that confirmed his feelings on serious relationships.

Brett's brows creased in confusion as he glanced from Hudson to Tripp. "What the hell is Hudson talking about? Did you meet someone at the clinic on Saturday and hook up with them?"

"No, he ran into an old flame at The Back Door after our afternoon at the clinic," Hudson said, once again speaking before Tripp could respond. "A gorgeous, stunning blonde. And when I left the two of them, things looked *very* promising. I was just hoping, for Tripp's sake, that the promise panned out and he got lucky."

Sure, he did, Tripp thought, leaning against the counter and attempting to tamp down his annoyance. He knew damn well if things hadn't turned out well with Skye, Hudson would have wanted her number. His intentions wouldn't be for more than a fling but that wasn't the point.

"Yes, we had a *great* evening together, and she spent the night."

"Bummer for me," Hudson joked, confirming Tripp's suspicions.

But Hudson wasn't an issue. His and Skye's unexpected morning after conversation was. Her desire to have a child had definitely thrown him, though he had no regrets about offering to be her baby daddy. But in all honesty, Tripp was harboring a bit of anxiety that she'd reject his offer and decide to go through the process without his involvement. *That* decision would fucking kill him as it meant he'd lose her for good. Not to mention, watching her belly swell with another man's baby, a *stranger's* baby, when he was willing to give her everything she dreamed of, would gut him.

"Are you going to see her again?" Hudson asked.

"Yes." He glanced at his friends, knowing he needed someone to talk to—because this wasn't a topic he was ready to discuss with his brothers. It would freak them the fuck out, then his mother would sniff out that something was wrong and press them for information, and Tripp didn't want her involved, either. Not unless Skye agreed to his proposal.

So he had no choice but to toss out the bombshell to Hudson and Brett. "And I might have offered to get her pregnant."

"You *what?*" Hudson asked, eyes wide.

Brett, meanwhile, rubbed his fingers against his temple. "You both are making my head spin. I feel like I'm missing a crucial piece of this conversation."

Hudson chuckled. "You're not alone. When I left Tripp and Skye at the bar, there was no mention of knocking her up."

Hudson was such a wise-ass, but at least the other

man was able to interject some humor into the situation, and Tripp appreciated the levity.

Since their time was limited before patients started arriving, Tripp gave them a quick rundown of the conversation he'd had with Skye yesterday, along with some background about their past. And because he still had strong feelings for her, that as soon as she'd mentioned *insemination*, there had been no doubt he wanted this to be *their* baby.

"Are you sure this isn't just a way to get back into her good graces?" Hudson asked, his tone skeptical.

"Definitely not." Tripp wasn't surprised by the question considering his friend's feelings on committed relationships after being burned by his ex-wife. Not that Hudson was painting Skye with that same brush, but no way would he understand Tripp's sudden need to be the man to make Skye's dream become a reality.

"So, what is this going to be . . . a business transaction?" Hudson asked as he braced his backside against the counter. "A wham, bam, thank you for your sperm, now let's go live our separate lives while raising a child together?"

Tripp hated how impersonal that sounded, considering his feelings for Skye were anything but. "Honestly, that's not my end goal. I want this baby, and I want Skye, too. There's no one else I'd want to build a life and a family with. For me, they'd be a package deal."

Not that he'd told Skye as much, because if she

were aware of his intentions, he knew it would be a deal breaker. From what he'd noticed, and all she'd told him, she wasn't mentally or emotionally ready for a committed relationship after her ex. And she would certainly have reservations about trusting the guy who'd walked away once before.

Those regrets would always haunt him, and there was nothing he could do to change the past, but he couldn't convince her of that in the short window he had before she went through with the insemination. His only chance was to convince her he was her ideal baby daddy. Once she was pregnant, he'd have time to step up and prove he was the right man for her, too.

Brett took a drink of his coffee, considering everything Tripp had just said before replying. "I take it she's not on board with your idea?"

"Not yet," he admitted. "She's been through some shit with her ex and is very guarded."

Brett nodded. The more thoughtful of the trio, he would be the one to understand Skye's reservations. He had married his high school sweetheart, and they'd been blissfully, happily married, until she'd died from ovarian cancer almost seven years ago, devastating him. He was raising his teenage daughter alone, had yet to date anyone seriously, and swore he'd never get married again.

The sounds of female chatter and laughter drifted from the reception area, telling Tripp the front end staff had arrived. It was time for them to get to work.

"Sounds like you have a lot to think about," Brett

said, as he refilled his coffee. "You know we're here to listen." *Even if we can't understand,* went without saying.

"What he said." Hudson shook his head and took his turn to refill his mug, then they all headed out of the break room.

Hudson was by his side as they started down the corridor toward their individual offices. "So, how is you being auctioned off at the charity event going to work? I mean, if this is something you really want with Skye, then dating another woman, even for an obligatory weekend, defeats your goal of being a stand-up guy."

Yeah, Tripp had spent all Sunday afternoon wondering the same thing. "I can't cancel. My sister-in-law would not be happy with me, which in turn would piss off my brother, Beck," he said, stopping in front of his office. "So, I came up with an alternate plan."

Now, he just had to hope he could persuade Skye to go along with his idea.

✧   ✧   ✧

SKYE WAS EXHAUSTED. It was Thursday afternoon, and with only two days left until the fundraiser gala, everything was coming down to the wire in terms of getting things coordinated with Future Fast Track, the charity event, and decorating and setting up the ballroom to their specifications. They also needed to make sure the Meridian did their share of marketing, as well. With Jade out on maternity leave, they'd been working long days, and even with assistants doing the grunt work, she and Lauren were still insanely busy.

But being inundated with work didn't stop her from thinking about Tripp, his offer, or their night together. Even if she'd wanted to put those thoughts out of her head, he'd made certain to keep in touch. He'd texted her all week, all day and each night, but not once had he pressured her for any kind of answer. Instead, their messages had been light and fun and flirty. They'd discussed their days—which gave her insight into Tripp's dedication to his job as a pediatric surgeon and showed her just how compassionate and caring he was when it came to dealing with kids. They spent the time getting to know one another again, and what she learned about the man Tripp had become, she really liked . . . more than was wise.

When they weren't texting, she was thinking of him, and would catch herself smiling like a schoolgirl with a crush . . . and that posed a problem. Because no matter how hard Skye tried to ignore her attraction to Tripp, or the flutters in her stomach that took flight every time her phone pinged with a text, it was getting increasingly harder to do. Tripp was just that charming.

"Knock, knock," Lauren said, interrupting Skye's distracted train of thought.

She shook her head. She should be working yet she couldn't stop thinking about Tripp and her future. Glancing up, she smiled as her co-worker strolled into her small office carrying two iced coffee drinks.

"It's time to take a break, and I think a shot of caffeine is in order to get us through the rest of the day. So, here you go." Lauren set Skye's favorite iced caramel macchiato on the desk. "Might as well enjoy that rush while you still can," she said meaningfully.

Skye laughed, knowing her friend was alluding to her getting pregnant at some point and being deprived of caffeine. "Thank you. The adrenaline kick is much appreciated."

She took a long sip of the cool drink, while Lauren plopped herself down in one of the chairs in front of Skye's desk with a tired sigh. "So, have you made a decision about Tripp yet?"

Skye had told Lauren about her weekend almost as soon as she arrived at work Monday morning. After so much time alone, she felt lucky to have a girlfriend in her life again and Lauren was the one person she could really open up and talk to without feeling judged or having to hold anything back.

Though she'd gone to lunch with her brother at the beginning of the week and had been tempted to tell him about Tripp and his proposal, she hadn't known how. Normally, she could tell Spencer anything, but her brother had never met Tripp while they'd dated. And considering how protective he was of her now, she didn't need him hunting Tripp down and pummeling him for propositioning his baby sister.

Skye sighed. "Not yet. Like I told you, he made his case with so many points, I promised him I'd think it over and get back to him." She also owed it to herself to consider his offer. "I'm just so torn."

Lauren nodded in understanding before sipping on her Frappuccino. She remained silent, giving Skye time to pull her thoughts together.

Back in the day, it would have been an incredibly easy choice, but with one failed marriage behind her, and unable to forget how Tripp had broken her heart, embarking on such an intimate, life-changing journey with him scared her. She couldn't deny she still had strong feelings for Tripp but after divorcing Jack, she'd vowed that she'd never depend or rely on any man ever again.

But this decision wasn't only about her heart, or her emotions. This was about being practical and smart. It was about looking out for her baby's welfare and future. Her reactions to Tripp's teasing texts and learning about him now reminded her too much of how she'd fallen hard and fast for Tripp the first time. If she agreed to let him father her baby—and that was a big if—she had more at risk than just her heart. She had her baby to think about and if things didn't work out again, she'd hate to subject her child to parents who were awkward around one another or worse, didn't get along.

Letting out a big sigh, she then took a long sip of her drink, drowning her confusion in sweetness and caffeine.

Lauren shot her an understanding look. "If you're undecided about what to do, let's break this down, shall we?" she asked, and relaxed more fully in her

CARLY PHILLIPS & ERIKA WILDE

chair.

"Sure." Skye would take clarity wherever she might find it. "I'd love to hear your thoughts."

"I know you've already considered the baby's health and genetics and obviously you'd know exactly what you'd be getting with Tripp." Skye nodded in agreement before Lauren continued. "But if you went the sperm donor route, then you'd have to trust what was filled out on the application. And honestly, wouldn't you want your baby to have a father figure in his or her life?"

That question had already crossed Skye's mind, and she had a ready answer. "I have two brothers who can provide that."

"Not the same thing," Lauren said with a frown and a shake of her head. "Let me phrase this a different way. Do you want your son or daughter growing up, asking about their dad, and you eventually having to admit you didn't know because you used some random guy's sperm to get pregnant?" Eyebrows raised, she shot Skye a knowing look and Skye cringed.

"That sounds awful," she admitted, unable to deny Lauren's point was a solid one.

How would her child feel not knowing anything about their father? That he'd been nothing more than a list of traits and attributes she'd selected from a catalog of strangers, when she knew she had the choice to offer them a good, solid man like Tripp? Worse, they'd have no connection to a paternal figure who could give them so much. She rubbed her palms against her eyes, the beginning of a headache coming on.

"I mean, you could always lie and say that their father died, but that comes with its own set of emotional trauma for a child." Lauren offered another option, as awful as the first.

Skye winced again. "I'd never lie to my son or daughter." And she didn't like how selfish it sounded for her *not* to give her child the memories and experiences of a loving father in their life.

Still, that had been her original plan and she met Lauren's gaze. "I'd be able to tell my child I wanted them so much I was willing to do it that way and raise them on my own," she said, trying to justify making that choice instead of Tripp.

Lauren nodded. "But they'd be missing all the things other kids would have. Father's Day, a father coaching a sport they were into, a dad at a father-daughter dance ... Look, if insemination were your only choice, none of this would make a difference. You'd love your baby with your whole heart," Lauren said.

"And they could still grow up feeling as though they were missing a crucial part of who they were." Which would be on Skye and her choices.

She swallowed hard as Lauren's smart words put everything that was truly important into perspective. No matter what, Skye wanted her child to be confident, secure and loved. She never wanted them to question their identity or search for answers they'd never find.

"So, I think the defining question would be, if you were going to have a baby with anyone, would you consider Tripp as the father?" Lauren asked. "Does he have *all* the attributes and traits you're looking for in a donor?"

"Yes." Skye didn't even have to think about her reply, because she knew Tripp was everything she'd look for in a father figure for her child. Not just his genetics, but who he was as a person. Kind. Encouraging. Supportive.

Lauren smiled brightly as she stood up. "Then it looks like my job here is done," she said simply, as if she'd untangled Skye's complicated situation and then wrapped it all up in a neat and tidy bow.

And she really had.

"Now that I've imparted my sage advice and you know what choice to make, it's back to work for me." Her wise friend turned to leave.

"Lauren, wait."

She turned, tipping her head curiously.

"Thank you," Skye said. "I mean it. This conversation was ... enlightening." And everything she'd needed to hear.

Lauren treated her to a warm smile. "Any time, Skye. I mean it."

As she watched Lauren leave the office, Skye accepted that her friend *had* helped to solidify her decision.

A sperm donor was easy and simple and uncomplicated . . . for her. But it was her child's welfare and emotional stability that mattered the most, and he or she deserved every advantage of being raised and loved by two parents and all they both had to offer a child. Even if in an untraditional way.

Knowing she had a man who was offering to give her the child she wanted, while also being a part of the kid's life was the best of both worlds and an ideal solution when that man was Tripp. There was no one she trusted more to be her baby's daddy.

That said, she was well aware that choosing Tripp would mean emotional entanglements she wasn't ready for. She picked up a pen and tapped it on the desk, pondering the best way to deal with her own anxieties over the arrangement when the thought came to her. The only way she could avoid emotional complications was to insist on a few stipulations. One that laid out strict rules, both about the baby making process and the joint custody terms that made them both comfortable before they dove in.

Now that she had an answer to give him, it wasn't something she wanted to discuss over a text. She wouldn't see him until the charity event on Saturday, which gave her time to come up with the parameters she needed before going into their new venture together.

Besides, she needed to get used to the changes that were in her future. She'd wait until after the event and give him her answer then.

Chapter Six

FINDING AN OPPORTUNITY to get Skye alone at the charity event was not an easy feat for Tripp. As one of the Meridian's event planners, along with Lauren, she was constantly moving around the room to make sure everything was running smoothly. He had attempted to talk to her a few times, but when it became clear that her mind was strictly on business, or she was being pulled in two different directions, he stopped trying because he respected that this was part of her job and he didn't want to interrupt or distract her.

So, he killed time visiting with friends during the reception hour, then eating dinner with Drew, Beck, and Chloe—all while keeping an eye on Skye, which was more a treat than a chore considering how stunning she looked in a silky, dark purple dress that skimmed all those sexy curves he'd enjoyed the previous weekend. She'd worn her hair down in soft waves, and he couldn't stop thinking about how those strands felt tangled around his fingers while he'd moved inside her. It had been a week since he'd last seen or touched her, and he was dying to get his hands on her again.

Hopefully, she'd give him that opportunity.

While dessert was served, Tripp continued to watch Skye and waited for an opening to approach her. Meanwhile, he absently listened to Drew and Beck discuss a real estate venture Beck was considering. Usually he joined in on the conversation, but he couldn't do that *and* still keep Skye in his line of sight.

He ate a bite of his chocolate torte and caught his sister-in-law looking at him. Judging by the slight arch to Chloe's brow and the quirk to her lips, she must have seen him staring at Skye, but much to his relief she didn't say anything in front of his brothers. The last thing he wanted to do was answer their nosey questions.

But time was running out to talk to Skye and the bachelor auction was due to start shortly. If he didn't find a moment to speak to her alone, he was going to end up with a date he didn't want.

Finally, he saw her go to the bar, and the bartender gave her what looked like a glass of water. She stood off to the side, sipping on the drink, and Tripp took that as his cue to finally speak to her.

Since his brothers were engrossed in their conversation, he stood up, and neither sibling even noticed. He didn't bother telling them where he was going, but he was certain that Chloe's gaze would follow him, if only out of pure curiosity.

He quickly made his way over to Skye, relieved that something else hadn't yet pulled her in another direction, though time was limited since it was announced that the auction would be starting soon. Skye's eyes lit up when she saw him, and a genuine smile touched her lips as he approached.

It took monumental effort to keep from taking her in his arms and kissing her, but he somehow managed to stifle the impulse. "Are you still working?" he asked instead.

She shook her head. "Actually, I've got a bit of a break until after the bachelor auction is finished and things wind down." She finished off the last of her water and placed her glass on a passing tray, her eyes taking him in. "You look very handsome in your tux, by the way. I'm sure you're going to raise quite a bit of money for charity tonight and make some lucky woman very happy."

He groaned, dreading the whole process when the only woman he wanted happy was her. Even though Skye was keeping their conversation light and teasing about another woman winning him, there was just enough reservation in her eyes to indicate that she was envious of the possibility, which worked to Tripp's advantage.

"I need you to do me a huge favor," he said, getting down to the reason he'd sought her out before the auction actually started and he lost the opportunity to convince her to bid on him.

"Okay," she said warily, clearly not knowing what to expect.

He grabbed her hands, holding them in his and

making sure he had her full attention. "I want you to bid on me and win, no matter how much it costs."

Her eyes widened in surprise. "Tripp, I can't do that. I don't have that kind of money to spend."

"I do," he insisted, more than prepared to shell out any amount as a donation. "The last thing I want is to spend an entire weekend with any other woman, so you'd be doing me a real solid."

She continued to stare at him, her shock evident, but eventually a playful sparkle glimmered in her eyes. "Does that mean *I* get to spend the weekend with you?"

The fact that she was more agreeable than he'd anticipated surprised him, but also gave him hope. "Do you *want* to spend the weekend with me?"

She bit her bottom lip nervously and nodded. "I was thinking we could use the time together to make a baby."

It was his turn to gape in shock as she delivered her decision, seemingly accepting his offer. "You're serious?" he asked, just to confirm that he hadn't misunderstood her.

"Yes, I'm very serious," she said with a soft laugh, looking so earnest, no doubts or uncertainties in her eyes or her expression. "I want you to be my baby daddy."

Elation surged through him. If they'd been any-where but in a room full of people, he would have wrapped her up in his arms and spun her around to express his excitement. He had so many other questions to ask, but another announcement came over the speakers for the bachelors to head to the stage, leaving him no choice but to leave her for now.

But it didn't matter, because Skye was going to have his baby, *their baby*, and it was the first step in winning her back for good.

✧   ✧   ✧

SKYE ACCOMPANIED LAUREN as the two of them headed toward the stage for the bachelor auction. Initially, she'd intended to give her friend moral support while Lauren bid on one of the men to pose as her fake boyfriend at her sister's upcoming wedding, but now Skye had her own agenda, as well.

"So, I told Tripp yes to his offer," she said as they waited for the auction to begin, along with a lot of other eager women. "And he asked me to bid on him, no matter the amount, so that he wouldn't have to spend the weekend with any other woman."

Lauren grinned and looped her arm through Skye's. "That's because he's a stand-up guy with morals and integrity. I mean, why would he want another woman when he has you?"

Skye's face warmed at her friend's words, but she rolled her eyes. "He doesn't *have* me."

Lauren waggled her brows playfully. "Well, technically he will be 'having you' for the foreseeable future until you get pregnant."

Okay, she couldn't argue with that, and maybe

there *was* a part of her that was looking forward to the fantastic sex they would have to make a baby. Now that her nerves about telling Tripp "yes" had dissipated, she felt much more relaxed. And then there had been his reaction to her announcement, how genuinely excited he'd been, and the entire decision felt right to her. Now, she could just enjoy her time with Tripp, along with the baby making process, until she became pregnant.

Skye watched as all the bachelors took their place on the stage, but mostly her eyes remained on Tripp, who'd also found her in the crowd of women. His gaze met and held hers, and his smile was only for her, while his brother Drew spoke to the man standing beside him—Derek Bettencourt, she believed his name was. Having Tripp's sole focus and attention released another round of those fluttering butterflies in her stomach.

Quickly, she scanned the other men up for bid, then glanced at Lauren, who was also taking inventory of the bachelors. "Okay, so which guy did you decide on for yourself?" she asked her friend.

A slight frown creased Lauren's brows. "His name is Neil Pierson, and according to the information he sent in, he's an accountant. I decided to go for someone boring but dependable who will hopefully be willing to fake date me at my sister's wedding and help convince my family I really *am* happy."

"Which one is he?" Skye asked.

Lauren's frown deepened. "In the brochure, he

was the last guy listed, but his spot is empty."

All the other men had taken their places, except for that last one, and Skye sought to reassure her friend. "I'm sure he's just making his way through the crowd to the stage."

Lauren nodded absently, then reached into the pocket of her dress and pulled out her cellphone. The device was on silent, but must have vibrated because Skye saw her check a text message that had just come in from "Mom".

"Crap, I need to call home," Lauren said in a panic as she glanced at Skye, genuine worry in her eyes. "Apparently, my grandfather had a mini stroke earlier this afternoon. My mom says it was mild and not overly serious, and he's already home from the hospital, but I need to hear for myself that he's okay."

"Of course," Skye said, nodding in understanding. "Go and call."

"Hopefully I'll be back in time to bid on the last guy," Lauren said, then rushed off to touch base with her mother.

Just as Lauren disappeared out of the ballroom, the last bachelor in the lineup finally—and very reluctant-ly—made his way onto the stage just as the auctioneer started to speak. And he certainly didn't look like the geeky, mild-mannered accountant Lauren was hoping for. No, this man had a grumpy scowl on his gorgeous face and looked as though he wanted to be anywhere but in a charity auction where he was a prize to win.

She had to stifle a laugh, because his gloom and

doom expression was certain to dissuade any female from wanting to be in his company.

Then Skye saw Billie, who worked for Future Fast Track and was in charge of the event, rush up to the far end of the stage and motion at the cantankerous guy until she had his attention.

"Smile, Chase!" Billie yelled at him, loud enough for Skye to hear.

His name was Chase, not Neil. For some reason Lauren's choice had been replaced with this gem of a guy.

Chase attempted a smile, but it looked more like a pained grimace.

Hoo boy, Lauren was going to have her hands full with that one if she made it back in time to bid on him. And most likely, her bid would go unchallenged because who wanted to go out with a stick in the mud like him? No matter how good looking he happened to be.

The auction started, and Skye refocused on Tripp, who wouldn't look at any other woman but her as the first few men were bid on, then walked off the stage to meet with their winners. She'd been so entranced by *this* man's sexy smile and seductive eyes that she had no clue how much the other bachelors sold for, which really didn't matter because Tripp had given her carte blanche when it came to winning him.

Skye started the opening bid on Tripp, and a few other women quickly topped her amount. Pure determination, and yes, a hint of jealousy, had Skye calling out higher numbers every time someone tried to steal Tripp from her. Okay, it wasn't stealing, she admitted to herself, but as she battled it out with the other ladies to win him for herself, she felt more territorial than she probably had a right to. But now that she'd decided to let him be her baby daddy, they were going to have a lot of sex in order for her to get pregnant, and there was no way she would allow another female to spend an entire weekend with her man.

Her man. She blinked at her possessive thoughts, then found herself bidding again.

The amount kept increasing . . . ten thousand, fifteen thousand, and higher. Every time someone topped her, she immediately shouted out a larger number. She couldn't help but feel a stab of guilt for spending his money so frivolously, but instead of looking upset by the accumulating amount, Tripp seemed amused, an approving smile on his face, which helped ease her conscience.

Gradually, the other ladies dropped out and stopped challenging her bid, which topped out at twenty-six thousand dollars. Then she was the last woman standing and holding the final bid. She grinned up at Tripp as the auctioneer banged his gavel and announced her as the winner, then instructed her to meet her bachelor out in the greeting area.

All at once, the adrenaline wore off and Skye swallowed hard when she realized how much she'd spent. While she was slightly horrified that the number had escalated so high, Tripp didn't even flinch. Instead, he winked at her, then strode off the stage.

Lauren still hadn't returned, and Skye hoped that everything was okay at home with her friend's family and grandfather. Not sure when or if Lauren would be back, Skye made her way out to meet Tripp. She found him in a sectioned off area with other bachelors and their winners, and she couldn't help but grin as she approached him.

"Congratulations," he drawled when she reached him, the low, husky sound of his voice and the way his eyes slid down the length of her, and back up again, making her breathless. "Is it wrong of me to say that your determination to win really turned me on?"

She laughed in an attempt to ignore the way her nipples tightened and heat pooled low in her belly. An instantaneous response when it came to this man. "That's what you get for giving me free rein with your money," she teased, then bit her bottom lip, truly feeling contrite. "I'm really sorry about that astronomical amount."

He shrugged and shoved his hands into the front pockets of his tuxedo slacks. "You're worth it. And it's all for charity and it's going to a good cause so I really can't complain."

He was so casual about the money, which told her that finances were not an issue for Tripp, as they were for her. When she divorced Jack, in order to expedite the process she'd asked for nothing of monetary value, which hadn't helped to speed things up at all since her ex dragged out the proceedings for as long as possible.

Still, in the end she'd been awarded a small settlement, which had been just enough for her to start out fresh and new and have a bit saved away for the insemination process. Now, she was grateful that she could put that money toward other things for the baby.

Tripp tipped his head to the side as he regarded her curiously. "So, now that we're definitely doing this baby thing, what changed your mind about us having a child together?"

"You," she said simply. "Because I know the kind of supportive, encouraging father you'll be, especially after listening to you talk about your young patients and how compassionate and capable you are with them. And I think it's important that a child has their biological father in their lives. There's also the fact that I know we can be friends as well as co-parents. And most importantly . . . I trust you and the man you are."

"Yeah, trust is important," he murmured, and gently brushed a stray strand of hair away from her cheek.

She shivered at his touch, wanting more, and had to remind herself that this wasn't a courtship between them, but a mutual agreement to share a child. No emotional or romantic entanglements involved. Hopefully. And that meant she had to be the one to establish those boundaries as soon as possible before she did something incredibly stupid . . . like fall in love with him all over again.

She exhaled a breath. "We need to set rules about how this arrangement between us is going to play out."

He frowned, not looking thrilled at her request or mention of rules. "Such as?"

Her list was . . . complicated, and it wasn't a conversation she wanted to have with other people around. "I don't think tonight is the time or place to discuss those terms, so why don't we both think about what we really want and expect out of this agreement, and how we want to handle the sex part, as well."

A slow, wicked grin lifted his sensual lips and his eyes darkened. "I don't think either one of us has an issue with the sex part of this agreement. We both know what we're doing and that we're good together. Sex will be the fun, very enjoyable part of this arrangement."

She felt her cheeks warm, which was ridiculous considering all the dirty things this man had done to her body the week before. "There's more to it than just sex," she said, trying to keep this as business-like as possible, which was important to keep those boundaries established. "I mean, yes, we'll be having sex. It's the *when* we'll be having sex, but I'll explain all that later. How about we discuss the specifics over dinner at my place tomorrow night, around six?"

"Sure," he said, and that devilish smile remained.

Despite his easy going response and seemingly laid back attitude, she caught the glimmer of a challenge in his eyes, and she had to admit that confidence caused a bit of concern. She knew from experience how persuasive and charming Tripp could be, how when he set his sights on something or someone—namely her—

that her own willpower had a way of crumbling beneath his determination and fortitude.

Yes, sex and making a baby would be the easy part of this arrangement, but resisting Tripp and his persuasive tactics would require far more restraint. Already, based on their one night together and a week of getting reacquainted over texts, she could feel an emotional pull toward him, which made those boundaries and rules that she planned to establish between them all the more important. She intended to make it clear that while she had no issues giving him free rein with her body during the process, her heart was off limits.

From inside the ballroom, she could hear the bachelor auction wrapping up, which made her wonder what had happened with Lauren. After promising to text Tripp her address for dinner the next evening, she headed back inside the ballroom in search of her friend.

The auction was over, the crowd of women around the stage dispersing, since there were no other men left to bid on. Catching sight of Lauren, Skye waved her down.

"Hey, how is your grandfather?" Skye asked, unable to make sense of the range of emotions reflecting on Lauren's face. But at least she didn't detect any panic over her family situation, which relieved Skye.

"He's okay," she said, her brows creased with normal concern. "He had what's known has a transient ischemic attack. They ran blood tests and scans and

JUST A LITTLE PROMISE

there is no permanent damage, thank God. He's at home resting and he'll have to see his doctor on Monday, but my mother assured me he's going to be fine, and I don't need to rush home when I'll be there for my sister's wedding next month."

"Good. Did you make it back to the stage in time to bid on a bachelor?"

Lauren grimaced, shaking her head and finishing with a groan. "Yes, and I ended up with Mr. Grumpy Pants, and not Neil Pierson the dependable accountant I was expecting." She met Skye's gaze, dread swirling in the depths of her eyes. "By the time I got back to the ballroom he was the only one left and I just panicked and didn't let that scowl deter me from bidding on him. Not that I had much competition," she muttered.

Skye swallowed back a laugh since Lauren sounded so miserable. "What happened to Neil? Did the auctioneer say?"

"Apparently he got sick with the flu, so this Chase guy was his last minute replacement. Billie must have been desperate to find someone, because he did not look happy to be up on that stage. But at least I got him dirt cheap."

"Well, that's a plus, at least," Skye said with a smile, trying to be positive.

Lauren sighed. "I'm on my way out to the greeting area to meet him. Keep your fingers crossed that I can persuade him to accompany me to my sister's wedding next month for our weekend together."

"You've got this." In a show of support, Skye held up both hands, fingers crossed for double the luck. "Go dazzle him with your beauty and charm, and I'll handle checking in with the Meridian service staff to make sure everything is still running smoothly."

Her friend straightened her shoulders and smiled. "He doesn't look like the type to be bowled over by beauty and charm, but I'll certainly try my best."

Chapter Seven

TRIPP ARRIVED AT Skye's apartment in Brooklyn the following evening as scheduled, still unsure what "rules" she was about to enforce in regard to their baby making arrangement. But he was prepared to accept whatever formalities she thought necessary to make this feel like a safe venture for her.

He already knew he wasn't going to be thrilled with her restrictions and stipulations, but he suspected her reasons for establishing boundaries had everything to do with protecting her emotions. And if that's what she needed to feel comfortable with him and the situation, then for now he'd abide by those rules.

He knew enough about her recent past to understand how badly she'd been hurt by her ex, how cautious she was now with men, even if he still didn't know the details of what had happened. But if adhering to her conditions allowed him to build a foundation of trust and let her slowly lower those walls, then he'd bide his time, be patient, and agree to whatever she wanted . . . while systematically finding his own way to strip away her reserve and ensure she knew that he was invested in this relationship one hundred percent. For the baby they created together but also for Skye.

While he was freaking excited about the possibility of being a dad, the thought of having a real future with Skye had him determined to barrel through her defenses and prove to her that he was a man she could depend on in every aspect of her life.

He parked his car and once inside the lobby of the complex, he checked in with the doorman, who allowed him access to the elevator since Skye had added Tripp to her approved guest list. He pushed the button for the tenth floor, and once he arrived on her level he found her apartment and knocked on the door.

He heard her on the other side, looking through the peep hole then releasing the lock to let him in. The door opened, and Skye greeted him with a genuinely happy smile. She was wearing a cute, casual dress and a pair of sandals, and part of her wavy hair was clipped back, displaying her delicate features, pretty blue eyes, and pink glossy lips. She wore minimal make-up compared to the glamour of last night's charity event, but he honestly preferred this natural, fresh-faced version of Skye the most.

"Come on in," she said, waving a hand inside. "You're right on time. I just took dinner out of the oven."

It took all his control to resist the urge to greet her with a kiss—as if they were a true and romantic couple—and instead walked past her and into her place without touching her at all. The front living area was an open concept design, small but cozy, and decorated in a way that was warm and inviting.

He followed her into the kitchen, inhaling the scent of something savory and delicious while she headed to the stove top and served up what looked like baked chicken parmesan and a side of sauteed vegetables.

"What can I do to help?" he asked.

"There's a bottle of wine on the table," she said, nodding her head toward the small dinette that already had two place settings. "You can pour us each a glass."

Grabbing the chilled bottle of pinot noir, he did as Skye asked while she finished plating their meals then brought the dishes to the table. They sat down and started to eat. He didn't pressure her for the discussion he knew would come eventually, and instead just enjoyed her company, their relaxed, easy conversation, and the fantastic dinner she'd made.

Tripp could easily imagine that this is what it would be like to come home to Skye every night after work, and he wanted that intimacy with her so badly the thought caused a wistful pang in his chest.

When they were finished, she insisted he go and sit in the living room while she cleaned up and put away leftovers. Seeing the slight bit of nervousness in her eyes over the discussion ahead, he refilled both of their wine glasses and brought them with him, then made himself comfortable on the couch to wait for her.

He smiled when he caught sight of the *What to Ex-*

pect Before You're Expecting paperback on the coffee table, and reached for the hefty book to take a look inside. He skimmed through the six hundred plus pages, shocked to see how much information was packed into the volume—everything from getting into baby making shape, to fertility friendly eating, to how to pinpoint ovulation. There were plenty of pages dog-eared, mostly dealing with fertility treatments and the insemination process, which she no longer had to worry about.

He found himself perusing chapter seven more thoroughly, which was all about baby-making sex, from timing to positions to logistics, and how to keep it sexy and fun. As he'd told her last night at the charity event, Tripp didn't think they'd have any issues with that part of the process.

When Skye finally joined him fifteen minutes later, settling on the sofa beside him, he set the book back down and retrieved a folded piece of paper from his wallet, handing it over to her. "This is for you."

She opened the paper, a puzzled look crossing her features as she glanced at the report he'd printed out earlier that day from his primary doctor's patient portal. "What is this?"

"My latest physical and blood tests results showing that I'm in good health and clean," he said, wanting to give her that peace of mind. "And you're the only woman I've been with since I had this blood test."

She looked at the date on the document and her eyes widened in surprise. "Over four months ago?"

He shrugged. "What can I say? I'm all about quality over quantity these days when it comes to sex. I've only slept with two people since my last relationship ended nine months ago, and one of them was you."

She looked surprisingly . . . relieved. "Thank you for sharing this."

"Of course." He picked up both of their wine glasses from the coffee table and handed Skye hers. "I want you to know how seriously I'm taking this, and the last thing I'd ever do is put you at risk in any way."

"I appreciate that." She took a drink of her wine and settled back against the sofa cushions. "So, I've already done the fertility testing on my end since I was planning on getting inseminated, and my hormone levels and ovarian reserve for my egg supply are in the high range for fertility." She paused a moment, worrying on her bottom lip. "I know this is a lot to ask, but I'd like for you to get a semen analysis, just to make sure your sperm count is good and we're not wasting our time trying to get pregnant the old fashion way if there are any potential issues."

He hated the way "*wasting our time*" sounded, but understood her concern. It was best to know upfront that both of their reproductive systems were in optimal health—or that he wasn't shooting blanks, God forbid—even if the last thing he wanted to do was masturbate and ejaculate into a cup.

"Sure," he said with a nod. "I can get it done tomorrow so we can have the results in a few days."

She tipped her head to the side, surprise flickering

in her eyes. "That's a quick turnaround."

He shrugged. "I just need a doctor other than myself to order the lab test, which Hudson or Brett can submit for me, even if that means enduring their shit for what the semen analysis process entails."

She laughed lightly. "Yeah, sorry about that," she said, sounding more amused than contrite.

"So, let's talk about these rules of yours," he said, wanting to know what restrictions he was up against.

She exhaled a deep breath. "I don't want to blur the lines of what we're doing here, which is trying to get me pregnant. And the only way to do that is to only have intercourse to make a baby, when I'm ovulating."

Disappointment rushed through him. The fact that she'd ovulate only once a month meant he only had limited physical time with her. And it wasn't about having sex, but wanting them to get closer emotionally.

"No practicing, huh?" he teased before taking a drink of his wine.

She shook her head, and he didn't miss the regret that passed over her features. "For one, I don't want to waste perfectly good sperm on 'practicing', and, I'm not in a place where I can handle this arrangement getting emotional."

She paused for a moment, her gaze meeting his, enabling him to see the vulnerability in her eyes. "I care about you, Tripp. I wouldn't be doing this with you if I didn't, but after Jack, well . . . I already told you that I'm not looking for anything serious and the only way to keep this situation from getting complicated is to limit intercourse to those ovulation times."

Her request was frustrating for sure, but he saw her fears and knew they were real. Insisting on anything more between them would only cause her to retreat, or call off this whole deal completely, and that wasn't an option for him when his end goal included a future with her, as well. He understood her reasons for protecting herself, even if he didn't like it.

At some point, he had to get to the bottom of what happened with her ex, but tonight was not the night. Tonight, he was going to respect the fucking rules and boundaries because he refused to do anything to pressure her or break her trust.

She gave him a forced smile. "I think it's best if we think of this situation as two good friends making a baby together."

He almost grimaced, hating that particular label she put on them. He wouldn't argue, but his mind was already thinking ahead and trying to figure out how to skirt her little rule and find ways to slowly, gradually, establish more than a "friends with baby making benefits" relationship between them.

"Okay," he said, just to appease her for now.

She set her wine glass down on the table, then grabbed her cellphone and pulled up an app, her face now alight with excitement. "I've been tracking my ovulation cycle for the past six months, and according to my app, and having had my period this past week, my next window of opportunity is in about two weeks." She switched to a calendar and gave him the dates for that weekend. "Do you think we can plan on spending those days together?"

He thought ahead to his own schedule and realized that it conflicted with a work commitment. "I'm on call that weekend for the practice, but I'll get Brett or Hudson to cover for me."

She bit her bottom lip. "What are you going to tell them for needing the weekend off?"

"The truth," he said, and chuckled when her eyes widened in embarrassment. "They already know about me offering to get you pregnant, so it's not going to be a surprise or an issue," he assured her.

Her cheeks turned a warm shade of pink, and she pressed her palms to her face. "I can't imagine what they think of me and what we're doing."

He stretched his arm across the back of the sofa. Skye was sitting close enough that he was able to lightly skim his fingertips along her shoulders, and he didn't miss the way she shivered from his touch. "Well, Hudson already knows you're amazing and stunningly gorgeous, and as for Brett, well, he doesn't have an opinion since he hasn't met you. But when he does, he'll find you just as irresistible as I do."

She rolled her eyes and laughed before turning more serious. "Can we agree that we won't tell our families what we're doing until I'm actually pregnant? The last thing I want to do is explain the situation to them beforehand and answer a barrage of questions, or have them ask how things are going every time I see them. Once I'm pregnant, it's a done deal and no discussion will be needed other than telling them that we'll be co-parenting."

"That sounds fine to me," he said, which saved him from having those awkward conversations, too.

"Thank you so much for doing this for me," she said with an enthusiastic, smile.

She leaned closer and wrapped her arms around his neck, giving him a hug he knew was meant to express how happy she was. Instinctively, he returned the embrace, sliding his arms around her waist, but all he could think about was how her lush curves were now pressed against his body. His dick thickened as he inhaled the sweet, floral scent clinging to her skin, and he gritted his teeth against the flood of arousal that immediately coursed through his veins.

"I appreciate your help more than I can say," she whispered into his ear.

He held back a groan. She appreciated his *help*? The last thing he wanted was her goddamn gratitude for essentially being her stud. Before he could stop himself or truly think through his actions, he released a low growl of frustration, gripped her hips, and pulled her onto his lap so that she was straddling his thighs, her knees braced against his hips to keep her legs spread open.

She gasped in shock and jerked her head back, her eyes reflecting a myriad of confusion—and instantaneous desire—as he skimmed his palm up her bare thigh. "Tripp . . . you agreed," she said breathlessly, her skin already flushed. "No sex unless we're making a baby."

He was dying to touch her, and not out of fucking friendship. "I agreed to no *intercourse* unless we're making a baby," he corrected her, as his hand slowly dipped beneath the hem of her dress and traveled higher.

He was determined to make her lower those physical walls with him, which would hopefully lead to a more emotional connection. If she pulled back again, he'd let her go ... and try again another time. One way or another, he'd make this stubborn woman his and vanquish her demons in the process.

"So, technically, I'm not breaking any of your rules by touching you with my fingers," he continued. "I can at least make you feel good. Will you let me?"

Knowing he wasn't playing fair, and not really caring at this point, he followed up that question with a firm, dragging caress of his thumb along the front panel of her silky panties, which were already damp.

She moaned softly and pressed her forehead to his, already falling under his seductive spell. "It's not a good idea," she said, though her tone lacked any real conviction.

It wasn't a no, rather she was waffling and that was enough for him to keep going.

"Actually, it's a great idea and let me tell you why," he said, deciding to take a playful approach as he slipped his thumb beneath the elastic band of her panties and rubbed that finger against her clit, making Skye squirm on his lap and her pussy get wetter with each deliberate stroke.

"Orgasms reduce tension and stress, which are the last things you need when you're trying to ovulate and conceive. A satisfying orgasm helps you relax so you can get a good night's sleep, which is important for you and your body. Not to mention, they can help strengthen your pelvic floor muscles for pregnancy, and besides, orgasms feel damn good. So why not indulge and enjoy?"

She released a soft, little laugh tinged with amusement, her face still so close that her breath mingled with his. "So, is this your professional opinion on the matter, Dr. Daniels?"

"Umm, it is," he murmured huskily. "Are you convinced?"

"I shouldn't be . . ." She shuddered when he pressed down on her clit, her hips thrusting into his touch while her eyes darkened with undeniable need. "But if it's what the doctor ordered . . ."

"Yeah, it is," he replied, and before she had a chance to change her mind, he stretched them out on the couch so that she was half beneath him, with one of his thighs notched between her legs to keep her thighs apart.

Her breath caught at the unexpected move, and he lowered his head and kissed her before she could say a word. She put up zero resistance as her soft lips melded against his, opening in invitation, and he took what she was offering without hesitation. She reached up, her fingers tangling in his hair as his tongue slid against hers, exploring that sweet-tasting mouth deeply, hungrily.

He slid his hand into her panties, his fingers gliding through her slick heat, wetting them so that two digits thrust effortlessly into her body. Her back arched, and she whimpered against his mouth, her hips moving rhythmically as she shamelessly fucked herself on his fingers. The firm, circular motions of his thumb on her clit drove her wild, and she held nothing back as he pushed her toward completion.

This was exactly how Tripp wanted Skye . . . completely out of her mind with need for him and what he could give her. He was certain she believed that this was just about an orgasm, nothing more than pure pleasure, and that because his body wasn't connected to hers, the act was impersonal, clinical, even. That this was just about letting off a little steam.

But Tripp knew better when it came to Skye. She wasn't someone who could remain detached, who could compartmentalize any form of foreplay or sex as just a means of finding release—which was exactly what had happened all those years ago between them. Any form of physical touch would always mean something to her on a deep, intimate level, which worked to his advantage.

Tripp continued stroking her pussy and clit, his sole focus to make her feel desired. Wanted. And adored by him—something he doubted her ex ever took the time to do. *That* was the way to Skye's heart. Not the end result of a satisfying climax, but traveling the path of letting herself be vulnerable and trusting him to take control of her body and its responses. Getting out of her head, letting down her guard, and allowing those walls to crumble and fall away from her bruised and battered heart so he could find his way back in, and protect what he should have kept safe all those years ago.

Instinctively knowing Skye was close to the edge, he ended the kiss and lifted his head, staring down at her as she fisted her hands in his shirt, as if trying to find some kind of anchor to the storm about to sweep through her. Her eyes were half-mast and hazy, her face flushed with passion, and she started to pant as he pushed her even higher.

"That's it, baby girl," he praised in a low murmur. "Let go so I can watch you fall apart for me."

With a soft cry erupting from her throat, she tossed her head back and obeyed his order, her climax slamming into her so hard she shook with the intensity of it. Her body clenched around his fingers, reminding him how good it felt when he was buried deep inside of her and she came around his cock.

His dick throbbed in response, almost to the point of pain, but this wasn't about his pleasure. It was about building trust and intimacy with Skye, and he was fairly certain he'd achieved his goal for tonight.

But in two weeks, when he had her all to himself for a weekend, all bets were off.

Chapter Eight

THE FOLLOWING TWO weeks passed quicker than Skye expected. A few event contracts at The Meridian kept her busy during the day with marketing and meetings. And while she'd made it a deliberate point *not* to see Tripp in person in the evenings because she didn't want to chance a repeat performance of their last time together, he insisted on FaceTiming her every night once they were both home from work and settled in for the evening.

It didn't help matters that she couldn't forget about that moment on the sofa, and how he'd found a way to bend her rules—or the fact that she'd *let* him. The man was so flirtatious, so charming and persuasive, he'd actually convinced her that she'd *needed* an orgasm for her mental health and physical well-being.

She had no one to blame but herself for giving into temptation, but she'd decided once he'd left her apartment that it would be a smarter idea to keep her physical distance from Tripp until their baby making weekend, since she didn't trust herself with him. One touch, and she was putty in his hands.

But she had to admit that he'd made it difficult for

her to keep her walls up emotionally. His check-in calls with her usually ended up being an hour or more conversation, mostly because he was so easy to talk to, and she honestly enjoyed his company. He made her laugh, he made her feel special, and whatever she wanted to talk about, interested him. For the first time in years, she felt seen and heard, and that what she had to say was important and meaningful to someone other than just her family.

Her attraction to Tripp was undeniably strong—that went without saying—but she loved the secure friendship they were establishing, too.

She'd also spent the past two weeks preparing for their weekend together. She'd meditated daily, went to her yoga classes, and was diligent about taking her prenatal vitamins. She met with her brother a few times for her kickboxing, and while he'd commented that she looked happier than she had in a long while, she didn't tell him about Tripp, even though she knew he was a big part of why she felt so optimistic about her life and future.

On the Friday of the weekend she planned to spend with Tripp, she'd requested half the day off, so she went into work early to get a few things done before heading home. At one in the afternoon, she cleaned up her small office and stopped by Lauren's to let her know she was leaving.

Skye knocked on her door before walking inside, smiling as her friend glanced up from her laptop and stopped whatever work she was doing. "I just wanted to let you know I'm heading out for the day."

"Lucky you," Lauren said, giving her a cheeky smile in return. "Dare I say you're glowing?"

Skye laughed then rolled her eyes. "That's because I'm ovulating. According to what I've read, that surge of estrogen makes your skin look smoother and brighter when you're fertile."

"Nice little benefit," she acknowledged humorously. "But I'm thinking that radiant look on your face has more to do with the anticipation of having great, anything-goes sex with Tripp for the entire weekend."

"Okay, maybe a little," she admitted. Yes, she and Tripp were on a mission to make a baby, but Skye had also given herself permission to enjoy the process of getting pregnant.

"I knew it," Lauren said triumphantly. "And I'm so envious. Not about the baby making part, but the sex part. It's been way too long since I've had any."

Skye tipped her head to the side, curious to know how things were going with the bachelor that Lauren had bought at the auction, who'd very reluctantly agreed to accompany Lauren to her sister's wedding. "How's the whole getting-to-know-you phase with Chase coming along?"

Her friend frowned. "Right now, I'm the one doing most of the talking because he's not a big conversationalist, so it's like pulling teeth trying to get information out of him so we can at least pull off being a believable couple." She huffed out a frustrated stream of breath and ran her fingers through her dark hair. "And he's like a brick wall when it comes to sharing personal stuff, so right now I know little to nothing about him besides his occupation."

"But you have to admit that he's a *gorgeous* brick wall," Skye said, pointing out the positive. "So at least he's not hard to look at and will provide you with nice arm candy at the wedding."

Lauren exhaled a long sigh. "Yeah, he really is hot and super sexy . . . and uptight." She cringed at that last description. "We only have a few more weeks until it's showtime, and in order for us to look convincing I'm going to have to get a pry bar to open him up."

Skye actually felt sorry for Lauren. "Good luck with that."

"Enough about Mr. Grumpy Pants," Lauren said, waving a hand in the air to dismiss the discussion. "Tell me, where are you and Tripp going for the weekend?"

"I honestly don't know," she replied. "I told Tripp I'd be fine staying at my place, or his. I mean, all we need is a comfortable bed to accomplish our goal, but he insisted that we get away from our everyday life so we could concentrate on relaxing and getting me knocked up without any distractions."

"Smart man." Lauren nodded approvingly. "Well, wherever you end up, enjoy your time together and good luck getting one of your fertile eggs pollenated."

Skye laughed, then left the office and headed home where she changed into a loose, flowing dress and low heels. Nothing fancy, but she didn't want to spend the weekend in her yoga pants and a tank top, as she normally would if she'd stayed home. She packed a small suitcase with clothes and toiletries, and included the sexy lingerie she'd bought on a whim a few days ago.

Yes, there was a distinct and clinical purpose to this weekend, but there was no reason why her time with Tripp couldn't be fun, too. Who knew if another round of baby making sex would be in their future. According to the results of Tripp's semen analysis, the quality and quantity of his sperm was exceptionally high. With her in the throes of ovulation, all the stars were aligned in her favor.

Her cheeks warmed when she recalled their discussion about his analysis report one evening over FaceTime. Tripp joked about the procedure and what it entailed, making fun of the awkward process of masturbating in a sterile room with the end goal of ejaculating. When she'd teasingly asked if he'd watched porn to *get him there*, he'd replied with, *all I had to do in order to come was remember how fucking fantastic it feels to be inside of you.*

Yeah, that response had left her breathless, filling her with anticipation of their upcoming weekend together.

Finished packing, Skye zipped her bag and rolled it out to the front room to wait for Tripp to arrive— which, according to the clock in the kitchen ought to be any minute. While she waited, she sifted through the pieces of mail from the past few days that she'd left on the dinette table. A few bills, a couple of normal advertisements, and what looked like a letter with her name and address typed onto a label.

Warily, she picked up the envelope, which was postmarked from Boston with no return address. Her parents and other brother still lived there, and every once in a while she received a forwarded piece of mail from her old address, but she instinctively knew this wasn't one of those.

Her stomach clenched with the kind of anxiety only one person had ever been able to incite inside of her, and the exhilaration of seeing Tripp faded as she forced herself to open the envelope, then unfold the single sheet of paper inside.

Her fingers shook and a chill chased down her spine as she stared at the picture of herself, sketched in black pencil. She immediately recognized the distinct style and characteristics of the drawing as only belonging to one person. Her ex-husband.

Jack was an excellent and talented artist. When she'd first started dating him, he'd drawn her all the time—mostly when she wasn't aware he was doing so. During their courtship when he'd been so affectionate and attentive, she'd thought it was an incredibly romantic gesture, but now, receiving a sketch of herself was creepy as hell.

Unease twisted in her belly and her throat went dry. There was no note or message attached, but the fact that she'd received this letter without a forwarding address label on the envelope meant Jack knew where she lived. It was a deliberate taunt to make her aware that he knew where to find her, even if they were a few hundred miles apart.

That quickly, old trauma resurfaced, threatening to overwhelm her.

Just a few minutes ago she'd been so happy and excited to see Tripp, and now, *poof*, all that enthusiasm was gone, replaced by an awful, sickening dread. She was so distracted and rattled by the picture and what it meant that when a firm knock sounded on the door, her entire body jerked in panic and the piece of paper slipped from her fingers and fluttered to the floor.

Her heart slammed against her chest, beating in double time, terror gripping her until the person on the other side of the door knocked again and she realized that it had to be Tripp.

With extreme caution and trembling legs, she walked to the entryway and looked through the peephole. Relief flooded her entire being when she saw him on the other side. She unbolted the lock and opened the door. Tripp's sexy smile greeted her, then immediately turned into a concerned frown.

"What's wrong?" he demanded, his gaze intense on her face, which probably showed every one of her distraught emotions.

"Nothing," she forced herself to say while trying to calm her racing heart. "I'm fine."

She hadn't been able to conceal the slight tremor in her voice, and Tripp's eyes darkened with skepticism. "Skye—"

"I'm *fine*," she insisted, cutting him off because she was desperate to get out of her apartment, which was now tainted by her ex's knowledge of her whereabouts. "Let's grab my bag and go, please. My suitcase is over there by the dinette table." She couldn't bring herself to look at that sketch again.

Tripp hesitated for a moment, his worry obvious.

"*Please*," she said in a strained, cracked voice.

He looked torn but then finally moved, walking over to her luggage, but when he arrived at the table, he stopped and stared at the open piece of paper laying on the floor, along with the envelope. He picked up both, reading the information printed on the front of the envelope, then looked at the drawing.

As if instinctively knowing the sketch was the reason behind her extreme reaction, he cast his gaze back to her. "Who drew this picture of you?" he asked calmly, which belied the flash of anger in his eyes.

God, this wasn't how she wanted to start their weekend, bringing Jack front and center—and boy, wouldn't her narcissistic, asshole of an ex have loved knowing he'd caused so much turmoil when she'd been about to have a fantastic time with another man.

Tripp clearly knew she wasn't okay, and as much as she didn't want to discuss where that picture had come from, she wasn't going to lie, either. "It's from my ex," she said, and forced herself to sound unaffected. "Somehow he found my address and mailed it here. Clearly, he's trying to intimidate me, even from Boston."

Tripp nodded succinctly, as if that's all he needed to hear to understand her distress and the situation he'd walked into. Jaw clenched, he crushed the piece of paper into his hand and shoved it into the front pocket of his jeans, probably so she wouldn't have to return home on Sunday and see it again.

Grabbing the handle of her bag, he rolled it back toward her and slipped his hand into hers, making her instantly feel safe and secure.

"Come on, let's get out of here," he said, and this time she didn't argue.

Chapter Nine

HOLDING SKYE'S HAND protectively in his and keeping her close to his side, they walked out of the apartment building, and he led the way to his parked car.

Tripp had no doubt she wasn't fucking *fine*. Far from it, and the fact that her prick of an ex had caused such a visceral reaction to a drawing that he'd mailed to her—a year after their divorce had been finalized—gave Tripp even more insight into just how vindictive and conniving the asshole was.

Jack clearly knew what he was doing, manipulating Skye and her emotions from afar, but the question was, *why now?* The timing of that letter didn't sit right with Tripp. Though he knew her ex lived in Boston, the fact that he'd chosen *now* to start sending her a random sketch—just to tell her he knew where she lived—was suspicious as hell.

There was no reason for her ex to contact her, except to terrorize her and remind her of his presence. But as intimidating as Skye found the picture, and as much as Tripp wanted to suggest she file an out-of-state order of protection against Jack, a simple sketch in an envelope without a name or return address wasn't enough proof. Jack would have to step up his game in order for him to pose an imminent danger against Skye.

Once they were in Tripp's vehicle, heading out of Brooklyn on the way to the city, Tripp glanced over at Skye, who hadn't said a word since leaving her place. Her hands were folded in her lap, and she was staring straight ahead, her complexion still pale. Her fear was still tangible, and fury vibrated through Tripp, as did violent thoughts of tearing Jack apart limb by limb, so he could never hurt Skye again.

Tripp was done postponing any conversation about her ex because Skye didn't want to talk about Jack, or her past with him. This unsettling incident changed *everything*. If Tripp was going to be a part of her life, then he had to know what kind of threat, if any, this asshole presented.

But he needed time to calm the fuck down and forced himself to stifle the urge to barrage her with questions and demand answers that would overwhelm her right now, as well as cause her to withdraw completely and shut him out. He had to proceed with caution and approach the conversation when they both weren't still in the heat of the moment. It was important that he created a safe space for her to open up to him, and once they reached their destination, he intended to do just that.

As he maneuvered through the one way streets of Manhattan, he reached across the console and took one of Skye's hands in his to get her attention. She finally glanced at him, making him desperate to erase that haunted look in her eyes, even for a little while.

"So, I know you work at The Meridian, but have you ever stayed there as a guest?" he asked her.

She shook her head and smiled, seemingly relieved to have something more pleasant to focus on. "Not only have I never had a reason to stay at The Meridian, but the hotel is also a bit bougie for my budget."

"Then you're in for a treat," he said, bringing the back of her hand up to his lips for a kiss while they waited at a red stoplight. "We're staying there for the weekend in one of their penthouse suites."

Her jaw dropped, clearly aware of how much those luxurious, spacious rooms went for a night at a five star hotel like The Meridian. "That's insane, and very unnecessary."

Tripp disagreed. All he wanted to do was spoil and pamper her for the rest of her life, but for now, a weekend would have to do. "You won me at the bachelor auction. Aren't I supposed to show you a good time?"

"I bought you on *your* dime," she reminded him with a laugh.

"Yeah, well, the last thing I want getting out is that I was a cheap date," he teased, pleased to see a small sparkle of happiness back in her eyes. "I figure The Meridian has all the amenities we could want or need. And if we feel like going out at any point, which I'm warning you won't be often because you're going to be naked for the most part," he added with a lascivious grin, "then we're in a centralized location with great restaurants nearby, and other things we can do."

Finally reaching the hotel, he pulled up to the drop off area. They got out of the car, and while Skye waited for him by the curb, he gave the bellman their room number and a generous tip to deliver their bags, then retrieved his ticket from the valet attendant before heading inside with Skye.

With his hand low on her back, he guided her past the front desk and through the lobby toward the elevators.

"Don't you need to check in first?" she asked curiously.

He shook his head and pressed the UP button. "I did that earlier, before I picked you up. We're all set."

They rode the elevator all the way to the top floor, found their suite, and walked inside the marbled entryway, where their suitcases had already been delivered. Her eyes went wide as she took in the luxurious living area and the French doors that opened to a balcony that overlooked New York City. With it being almost four o'clock in the afternoon, and the beginning of October before time changed, the clear, unobstructed autumn view was quite spectacular.

She strolled deeper into the room, taking everything in, and he gently grabbed her arm and stopped her before she could get very far.

"Hang on," he said, turning her to face him before sliding an arm around her waist and bringing her body flush to his. "There's something I need to do first to officially start our weekend together."

She remained perfectly pliant against him, which he loved, and placed her hands on his chest while arching a playful brow. "And what's that?"

He threaded his fingers through her silky hair and used the strands to tip her face up to his and hold her there. "This," he murmured, and settled his mouth on hers.

The kiss started slow and sweet but didn't stay that way for long. As soon as his tongue skimmed along her bottom lip, she immediately opened for him, inviting him deeper, and he didn't hesitate to oblige. She was so willing and eager, whimpering softly against his lips as her need escalated. The hands on his chest gripped his shirt, then started fumbling with the buttons to start undressing him.

As hard as his dick already was, and as much as Tripp wanted to take her to bed and fuck her senseless until she was completely spent and her earlier upset forgotten, he wasn't ready to jump right into sex with her when they had the entire weekend together. First things first, and his top priority was taking care of Skye mentally and emotionally before focusing on giving her the baby they *both* wanted so much.

Lifting his mouth from hers, he gently grabbed her wrists, stopping her frantic efforts before she ripped the buttons right off his shirt. "Not so fast, Ms. Abbott," he drawled huskily.

Disappointment flickered in her eyes and she

pouted adorably. "So that kiss was just a tease?"

He chuckled at how miffed she sounded. "That was a warm up with a helluva lot more to come later," he promised her, softening the rejection with a kiss to her forehead before releasing her. "When did you last eat something?"

She wrinkled her nose as she thought about his question. "I had a bagel for breakfast."

He gave her a stern look, not happy that she'd skipped lunch. "Clearly, I need to feed you so you have plenty of energy and stamina for the night ahead." He clasped her hand in his and led her toward the main bedroom and the adjoining en suite. "So, while I'm handling dinner, you're going to take a nice, hot bath and relax and destress."

She sighed longingly as they walked into the spacious bathroom with an enormous soaking tub and high end toiletries on the counter that included bath oils, a loofah, and other luxurious amenities. "That does sound lovely."

"Good." He turned on the faucet and began filling the tub with steaming water. "You get undressed and I'll be right back."

He left to retrieve their overnight bags from the entryway and brought them to the bedroom. He opened his and pulled out a gift wrapped box and headed back to the bathroom, inhaling the floral scented steam of whatever oils she'd put into the water. When he stepped inside, his mouth went bone dry as he looked at Skye, who'd stripped off all her clothes except for a pair of thong panties. With her facing the mirror, as she put her hair up into a messy bun atop her head, he had a delectable view of tiny strips of satin and lace bisecting the rounded cheeks of her smooth ass.

The palm of his hand itched to caress her scantily clad backside, or playfully smack her bare bottom, but he resisted the urge. "This is for you," he said instead, and set the package on the counter.

Her eyes flared wide in surprise as she took in the exclusive "La Perla" name etched on the box—courtesy of Chloe, who'd steered him in the right direction for women's lingerie. Skye turned toward him, her expression etched in both delight and shock, and if he thought her ass was distracting, then her perfect breasts had him nearly salivating.

"What is this?" she asked, running a fingertip along the pink ribbon decorating the box.

He mentally shook himself out of his lustful stupor. "*This* is the only thing I'm allowing you to wear while we're in this suite," he said, forcing his gaze back up to hers before he spun her around and fucked her right up against the bathroom counter like a goddamn caveman. "I've got a job to do this weekend, and I prefer easy access to your body, whenever I want it."

"Okay." A pink flush suffused her cheek. She was clearly aroused by his dominant attitude—and emboldened enough to skim her fingers along her cleavage, which caused her nipples to peak into hard, lickable points. "Are you sure I can't convince you to join me in the bath?" she asked seductively.

He groaned and pressed a hand to his straining cock, which did nothing to ease his throbbing erection. "The offer is tempting, but you need to be fed and I'm going to order room service. Any requests?"

"No cravings yet," she teased with a smile. "So surprise me."

He nodded, needing to get hell out of there before he forgot his purpose of relaxing her for the difficult conversation ahead—one he intended to have before they focused the rest of the weekend on getting her pregnant. He dimmed the lighting in the bathroom and closed the door behind him.

While she enjoyed her bath, he rolled up the sleeves of his shirt and called room service and placed their dinner order. When he'd checked into the hotel earlier that day, he'd also purchased a few other add-on items to create a seductive ambiance for the evening, which included a few dozen roses and petals scattered around the living room and bedroom, tapered candles for their table out on the balcony, and a bottle of Dom Pérignon Vintage Rosé on ice.

Tripp didn't consider himself an overly sentimental guy but by the time the waiter left the penthouse, there was a distinct, posh romantic vibe in the suite, like nothing he'd ever experienced or done for another woman. Which told him just how special Skye was to him. She deserved to be spoiled and treated like a queen . . . *his queen*, to be precise.

With everything in place, and not wanting their

meals to get cold—even though their plates were beneath a silver cloche to keep their food warm—he started back to the bedroom to get Skye, just as she walked out. He came to an abrupt stop, as did his heart, before his pulse kicked back into gear again.

She looked stunning with her hair now down in soft waves, the lightest amount of make-up on her face, and her skin flushed from her bath. He'd purchased the pale gray chemise Skye was now wearing online and it had been wrapped in a box when he'd picked it up at the store a short while later, but seeing the silk chemise on her now was sexy as hell. The silk fabric slid across her skin sensuously with the slightest movement, and the slit at her left leg, along with the hand embroidered lace at her bodice and hem of the gown, added to the sensual allure of the lingerie.

He wondered if she was wearing panties, because he deliberately *hadn't* bought the matching pair so she'd be naked beneath. It was a thought that was going to torture him all throughout dinner.

"You look fucking amazing," he said, using the only words he could currently find in his vocabulary.

She blushed, as if those kind of compliments were rare, then glanced down at the plush gray fuzzy slippers on her feet and wriggled her toes in them, which made him grin.

"Thank you for the cozy and warm slippers," she said, lifting her gaze to his, a smile on her lips. "I know they don't really go with the lingerie you spent a small fortune on, but they make me happy."

That's all that really mattered to him. "Full disclosure, I did consider buying you a pair of those sexy kitten heels with marabou feathers, but I'm not an entirely impractical guy and wanted you to be comfortable for the weekend, too," he said humorously. "And, I also remembered how easily your feet get cold indoors without slippers or socks on."

She struck a cute pose. "Well, good choice, because socks would have completely ruined the outfit."

He chuckled, even though he disagreed. She could have been wearing a burlap sack and she still would have turned him on. But he couldn't deny that the nightgown was a helluva lot more enjoyable to look at.

"Come on, let's get you fed," he said, taking her hand in his and leading her out to the balcony.

The slight ambient sounds of New York City could be heard, even from this top floor, but it didn't detract from the romantic atmosphere. The sun was starting to set, and while there was a slight breeze outside Tripp had turned the heat lamps on a short while ago to make sure she stayed warm. The table was small and intimate with rose petals and tapered candles. When she sat down on one side he removed the domes from their plates then settled into his chair across from her before pouring them each a glass of Dom Pérignon.

She took a drink of the vintage rosé and sighed. "A girl could get used to being spoiled like this."

"That's what the weekend is all about," he said with a flirtatious wink, though he'd spoil her for the rest of her life if she let him.

They ate their dinner, enjoying the delicious Chilean sea bass, sauteed vegetables and rice pilaf, and when they were done and she sat back with a satisfied and content sigh, Tripp decided it was time to broach the subject of her ex-husband.

He hated to shatter the tranquility of the evening, but the conversation was just too important for him to let it go any longer. If he and Skye were going to embark on parenthood together, then he needed to know that she, and any child they had together, were always safe and protected, and he couldn't do that without knowing what he was dealing with when it came to Jack.

As if instinctively sensing a shift in the air, she glanced across the table at him. Holding her gaze, he softly, carefully said, "You know I have to ask about Jack."

She visibly stiffened. "No, you really don't. I don't want to talk about my ex."

He'd expected that immediate guarded response. He also recognized the stubborn tilt of her chin and knew he was taking a huge risk of fucking up this entire weekend by pressing the issue. But he also knew, after witnessing her gut-wrenching reaction to Jack's passive-aggressive tactic, *not* having this discussion wasn't an option for him. Not any longer.

"Sweetheart, I'm not giving you a choice." He kept his tone calm and gentle, despite his resolute words.

Her lips pursed, and she stared at him almost angrily, as if that defense mechanism would dissuade him, which it didn't.

Instead, he pushed forward. "I'm not asking about your past with your ex to be invasive. I'm asking because as the man who is going to father a child with you, and be a part of your life, I need to know what happened with Jack and what he's capable of. The fact that he can still rattle you so badly just by sending you a drawing is a cause for concern."

"And that's exactly why he did it. To rattle me," she said bitterly, her fingers gripping the stem of her champagne flute way too tight.

He nodded in understanding, and when she didn't offer anything more, he persisted, trying a different approach. "I know this isn't a conversation you want to have, but it would mean everything to me if you would trust me with what happened. I need to know, Skye, because like you told me that first night at the bar, you're not the same girl you once were."

Tears shimmered in her eyes, and she turned her head, looking back at the city skyline.

She looked so vulnerable, and his chest tightened at the knowledge that if he'd never ended things with her back then, he could have saved her the pain and misery she'd gone through with Jack. His choices had changed a part of her life and future, and not for the better as he'd thought it would.

Reaching across the table, he took her hand in his, and while she let him touch her, she didn't glance back at him yet. Which was okay, because he knew she was listening.

"I would do *anything* to go back in time and do things differently with you," he said, his voice a bit hoarse with his own emotions. "But I don't have that choice and that's my regret to live with. But I do have the ability to be the best version of myself for you now, in whatever capacity you need. All I ask is that you open up and trust me because the last thing I would ever do is hurt you in any way. You have to know that."

She nodded and finally met his gaze, the lingering pain in the depths of her eyes feeling like a knife to his heart. "I do know that."

Her assurance relieved him and he gave her fingers a gentle squeeze. "And with us potentially co-parenting a child together, I don't want any secrets between us. I don't want to be blind-sided by something your ex might be capable of doing."

He watched as she swallowed hard and seemingly gathered her thoughts but didn't speak immediately. He waited patiently, because that's what she needed from him—his patience—and he was more than willing to give her the time she needed to dredge up what had to be traumatic memories and share them with him.

After a few long minutes passed, she finally pulled her hand from his, exhaled a deep breath, and spoke. "When I first met Jack, everything between us was great. Honestly, from our first date he said and did all the right things and swept me off my feet, and I was stupid enough to fall for his confidence and attention and the charismatic man he pretended to be, which I now know was nothing more than a lie."

Her eyes flashed with resentment and contempt over the other man's deceit. "I can look back with a clear mind and admit that I was hurting from our breakup, that I was incredibly vulnerable and so it was easy for me to get caught up in Jack's charming persona. I didn't see his attentiveness as obsessive and controlling at the time because he'd couch his actions as being romantic. And our courtship was a whirlwind. Within six months we were engaged, by a year we were married . . . and that's when he started showing his true character."

Tripp hands balled into fists on his thighs. He found listening to her story difficult because of his rage toward Jack that was already simmering beneath the surface. The man was clearly a master of manipulation, and Tripp could easily understand how a woman as sweet and guileless as Skye had been back then would have taken Jack at face value.

Now that he'd managed to get Skye to open up to him, it was as though she couldn't stop the outpouring of pain, as if sharing all the heartbreak and disillusionment of her marriage was like a cathartic release for her. She continued talking while he listened, painting a horrific picture of what her life had been like as Jack's wife. Certainly not the kind of fairytale she'd no doubt envisioned.

He learned how Jack had systematically isolated her from friends and family and how she'd made excuses for his behavior, while also pretending to those same people that she was happy in the marriage when she'd been completely miserable. How he'd stripped her of her self-worth and confidence, destroyed her resistance and morale, and how nothing she did was ever good enough for him.

In a pained voice, she told Tripp how she'd lived in a fog of uncertainty and self-doubt, and how he'd undermined her emotions as a way to invalidate her reality of a situation and question her own sanity. He constantly criticized her, accused her of being too sensitive, and made her feel insignificant. And when she tried to confront him on an issue, he'd twist things around and left her feeling as though she was the one at fault.

His heart nearly broke when she revealed that her life for two years consisted of living with anxiety and frequent panic attacks.

Everything she told Tripp pointed to classic signs of being gaslit, of Jack eroding her self-esteem to gain power and control over her. Skye was a smart woman, but she was also very trusting, and Jack had violated that gift in a way that was extreme and inexcusable.

Skye paused for a moment, staring off in the distance, her expression still lost in the past before she shifted her gaze back to Tripp and continued. "The second year into our marriage, Jack thought we were trying for a baby—at his insistence, not mine. As much as I wanted one, I knew I couldn't bring a child into our toxic relationship so I hid my birth control and kept taking it. Of course he blamed me for not being able to get pregnant and made me feel inadequate as a woman. At that point, I knew I had to get out of the marriage, but I was scared and didn't know how to leave him because he'd threatened me with bodily harm if I tried."

She shuddered at the horrible recollection, and it was all that Tripp could do to sit across from her and suppress his rage. "What made you finally leave him?" he asked, keeping his tone as neutral as possible.

As soon as she absently lifted her hand and touched her fingers to her cheek, Tripp's entire body tensed because he knew what had happened before she even spoke, that her ex had crossed the ultimate, unforgiveable, and reprehensible line. Still, Tripp braced himself for the details.

"I discovered he was having an affair," she said, her voice hoarse. "I had undeniable proof, so I confronted him, and he didn't like the fact that I wouldn't back down. I didn't cower from his intimidating tactics. I told him I wanted a divorce, and that's when he shoved me against the wall and punched me in the face. It was the first time he'd ever hit me. The first time *anyone* had ever hit me." She pulled in a deep breath. "I'd stayed with him through everything else but I knew that hit wouldn't be the last. So, the next day, while he was out of the house, I packed up my things, called my brother, Spencer, to come and get me, and left for good."

She'd lifted her chin, showing him that while her

ex had tried to break her, he hadn't succeeded. Her spirit might have been temporarily damaged, but she was no longer broken. She'd survived the abuse and persevered, even if the asshole had left her beautiful heart battered and bruised in the process.

Tripp scooted his chair out but didn't stand. Instead, he beckoned to Skye. "Come here, baby girl," he said softly, needing to hold her, to make her feel safe after that unpleasant trip down memory lane.

As if needing exactly what he was offering, she strode over and sat on his lap, snuggling against his chest and burrowing her face against his neck. He stroked his fingers through her hair and down her back, his protective instincts rising to the surface.

"I will never, *ever,* let anyone lay a hand on you like that again," he said fiercely, meaning every word.

"I won't let it ever happen again, either," she responded just as vehemently.

Her resilience made him smile and he gently kissed her forehead. "That's my girl."

Skye had come out stronger, which wasn't an easy feat considering what her prick of an ex had put her through. As awful as it had been to listen to her account of everything she'd endured, it gave Tripp invaluable insight as to why she was so wary and guarded. She'd clearly struggled to rebuild her confidence and self-worth, and trusting any man after that ordeal, and allowing herself to be that vulnerable again, would be difficult.

But tonight was a start.

Chapter Ten

THE LAST THING Skye wanted to do during this weekend with Tripp was discuss her shitty marriage to Jack. But now that she had, she couldn't deny that a part of her felt lighter, and freer. As though verbally releasing all those unpleasant memories had finally given her the ability to feel less vulnerable, and had crumbled some of those walls she'd built around her heart after leaving Jack.

Her parents and brothers had known things were bad with her ex—it was difficult to ignore the huge bruise and black eye he'd given her their last night together—but she'd never truly given them all the disturbing details. They'd already been worried about her, and she'd been embarrassed and felt so stupid that she'd allowed the mental and emotional abuse to go on for two long years.

After leaving Jack, therapy had definitely helped her understand that she wasn't responsible for her ex-husband's narcissistic personality or behavior, that she'd been manipulated by a master. But she'd even withheld some of the most awful, painful parts of her marriage from her therapist. Still, she'd managed to learn how to let go of that shame and humiliation.

But tonight with Tripp was different. She'd allowed another *man*, one she truly trusted, to hear about her foolish mistakes and greatest shame. She'd exposed the deepest, most personal pieces of herself, and while a part of her feared being judged for staying in a toxic relationship for so long, Tripp had offered only kindness, understanding, and support.

Being held in his arms so protectively, his big, strong hands gentle and soothing as they strummed up and down her spine, was everything. Until now, she'd forgotten what being cherished and adored even felt like. Tripp reminded her that there were good, honorable men still to be found, and he was one of them.

A slight breeze caressed her skin, and even though the heat lamps were still turned on, she shivered as the cool air made the silk of her chemise flutter against her body. All she wanted right now was Tripp's warmth, both of them naked and generating their own special brand of heat.

She lifted her head from his shoulder and gave him a sultry smile. "Let's go inside," she said, beyond ready to forget about her ex and focus solely on the one man who'd promised to give her what her heart desired the most. A baby.

They stood up, and she clasped his hand in hers and led them back to the living room. Usually it was Tripp who was in charge when it came to sex, him who led the way and she followed, but tonight he let her set the pace, as if sensing that's what she needed after baring her soul to him.

Tripp always made her feel sensual and desirable, and this evening was no different. Instead of taking him to the bedroom, she stopped by the sofa and turned to face him, and the lustful way he stared at her brought every one of those dirty, uninhibited impulses to life. All she wanted was to drive him a little crazy.

Kicking off her slippers, she stood on her tiptoes and pressed her lips to his. His hands settled on her hips, his grip strong, but she could feel him holding back and for now she'd let him hang on to his restraint. She deepened the kiss while unbuttoning his shirt, then shoved the material down his arms and off. As their tongues tangled sinuously, she unbuckled his belt, unzipped his pants, and worked his slacks and underwear over his hips until both fell to pool around his feet.

Once he'd toed off his shoes, removed his socks, and untangled himself from his clothes, she gave him a little push backwards, just enough to force him to sit down on the couch, completely, gloriously naked. His erect cock jutted up toward his stomach, making her mouth water for a taste as he encircled the thick shaft in his hand, giving it a slow, leisurely stroke while she watched.

She stepped closer, and with a lascivious grin curving his lips, he reached out with his free hand and skimmed the tips of his fingers up the inside of her thigh, his touch immediately causing her to shiver in anticipation.

But as much as she ached to feel those fingers sliding deep into her pussy, she playfully smacked his hand away. "I didn't say you could touch," she chastised him.

He arched a dark brow at her sassy tone. "Just checking to see if you're naked under there."

She slowly edged up the hem of the chemise to give him a teasing glimpse, framing her bare pussy in the expensive, hand embroidered lace for him to see. He licked his lips and groaned deep in his throat.

"Naked and ready," she confirmed huskily.

"C'mere," he ordered, his voice a low, dominant growl that made her sex clench with the instinctive need to obey.

Not this time, though. Instead, she shook her head, causing her unbound hair to cascade along her shoulders. "Not yet."

She settled on her knees in front of his spread legs, pushing his hand away from his cock so she could take over. She wrapped her fingers tight around his length, and he watched with hooded eyes as she leaned forward and took him into the wet heat of her mouth.

She licked and sucked his cock, slow and leisurely at first, reacquainting herself with the size and shape of him. Her tongue swirled over the tip, her teeth lightly scraped along the hard column of flesh, and she purred in delight when he slid his hands into her hair and gripped the strands, holding her head where he wanted as he fucked her mouth a little harder, a lot deeper. The head of his shaft filled her throat again, and again, until she was lost in the taste and feel of him.

His entire body shuddered as he gave her hair a tug of warning. "*Fuck*," he groaned, the low, needy sound sending a thrill through her. "You need to stop before it's too late."

She swallowed the salty, sticky fluid seeping from the tip of his cock, the flavor on her tongue completely intoxicating her. As much as Skye wanted to finish him off like this, having him release down her throat defeated the goal of why they were together for the weekend. She wanted every drop of his come deep inside her body.

Releasing his erection, she stood up, quickly removing the nightie so she was just as naked as he was. She meant to tease him a bit more, but his green eyes darkened in appreciation and his hands reached out, finally taking complete control as he tugged her forward and helped her to straddle his lap. Without any other foreplay—she was already dripping wet from sucking his cock—he notched the head of his dick at her core, then grabbed her hips and slammed her down onto his rigid, pulsing cock, until he was buried to the hilt inside her.

She gasped and cried out, the initial shock of pain ebbing into the sweetest, hottest pleasure as she rode him, wild and uninhibited. He dipped his head, his mouth latching onto her breast, his teeth scraping across her sensitive nipple before he sucked hard and deep and she could no longer think, only feel as both of them rocked and gyrated desperately against one another.

Skye gripped his shoulders, her head falling back and her spine arching as scorching hot passion engulfed her. Desire coiled tighter, low in her belly. His hands dropped down to her ass, squeezing and dragging her closer so there was no space left between their bodies. The friction against her clit sparked, sending hot, vivid sensations sweeping through her.

With one hand tangled in her hair, Tripp brought her mouth to his and kissed her—deeply, hungrily. His tongue plunged against hers and her breasts scraped against the light texture of hair on his chest, adding to the overload of need threatening to overwhelm her in the very best way possible. She wrapped her arms around his neck and whimpered against his lips, her lower body straining and rubbing erotically against his.

She wanted more. She needed more. And Tripp gave it to her.

The orgasm that finally crashed through her was enormous, stealing her breath while her inner walls clenched around Tripp's cock, milking and stroking his shaft until he issued a guttural groan that vibrated against her lips. His body jerked beneath hers, and she could feel the throb of his cock and the hot spurt of his release as he came long, hard, and deep.

She collapsed against him in a boneless heap. It was still early in the evening, but between their emotional discussion out on the balcony and their vigorous fucking now, Skye was utterly drained and exhausted.

"I can't move," she muttered, her face buried against his neck.

He chuckled and held her closer, tighter, against him. "Lucky for you, I've got great stamina. Keep your arms locked around my neck."

She did as she was told as he stood up, shocking her with his ability to do so with her draped against him, and she instinctively secured her legs around his waist, keeping their bodies still joined. "What are you doing?" she gasped.

He cupped her ass in his hands, effortlessly hanging on to her as he strode toward the main suite. "I'm taking you to bed and making sure nothing leaks out on the way. Every sperm counts."

She laughed, loving that he could be so light-hearted about the baby making process. Everything about it felt so normal and easy with him. But despite having bared her soul, she still held onto the remnants of the pain and her fortitude to be independent and not beholden to any man ever again. Tripp would be an amazing dad to their child, and for the first time she had the thought that she was truly glad that he would be a part of her life, so she had someone to share all the milestones with.

When they reached the mattress, he laid her down and immediately shoved a pillow beneath her hips, which according to her *What to Expect Before You're Expecting* book, allowed the sperm a better chance to swim toward the cervix and into the uterus.

She glanced up at him, trying to ignore how hot he

looked after their tryst in the living room. "How do you know about the pillow trick?"

"I did some reading up on the best ways to achieve conception," he said, then waggled his brows playfully. "Wait until you see the way I plan to fuck you tomorrow for the deepest penetration possible. I want to give my swimmers every fighting chance they've got."

She groaned at the thought, but she was smiling. The man was committed, she had to give him that. He left her on the bed and headed to the bathroom to clean himself up, then went to the small kitchenette where he grabbed a chilled bottle of water and returned. He made her take a few sips, and after about twenty minutes he removed the pillow then crawled into bed beside her.

She rolled to her side and he spooned her from behind, his arm tucked securely around her waist and her back aligned to his chest. She was tired, but more content than she could ever remember feeling, and it didn't take her long to fall into a deep, dreamless sleep.

Chapter Eleven

THE FOLLOWING DAY, after spending a lazy morning in bed with Tripp, followed by hot shower sex, then a leisurely breakfast, Skye was delighted when he presented her with an afternoon at the hotel spa. Much to her surprise, he'd purchased their most luxurious package, which included a manicure and pedicure, a facial, a massage, and a decadent body scrub and polish.

By the time she'd returned to the suite after a good five hours of pure indulgence, she felt relaxed, pampered, and rejuvenated. Her skin glowed and was smooth and soft to the touch, she smelled like honey and apricots and any lingering tension in her muscles had vanished. And just because she'd felt a bit daring, she'd had the nail technician paint her toes and fingers a vibrant shade of red.

When Tripp greeted her after her lavish spa day, her stomach grumbled hungrily. It was late afternoon, and he insisted they get out of the suite instead of ordering in again, so they decided to head down to the lounge for happy hour appetizers and a drink.

He changed into a pair of casual black slacks and

an olive green linen shirt, and she opted for a classic little black dress that was subtly sexy, showing just a hint of cleavage and leaving her legs bare. But the hot, hungry, appreciative way that Tripp looked at her when she walked out of the bedroom set her body on fire.

They arrived at the lounge early enough that they were able to grab a small booth off to the side near the bar. They sat side by side instead of across from one another, and after ordering a few appetizers and their drinks were delivered—a refreshing ginger-orange mocktail for her and a Macallan neat for Tripp—he moved closer to her.

"God, you smell good," he said, his tone husky as he nuzzled her neck, inhaling the scent of honey and apricots still lingering on her skin from the final spa treatment. "I just want to eat you up."

She shivered at the dirty connotation of his words, grateful that no one else could hear their private conversation. "Later, I promise you can eat whatever you want."

He lifted his head and smirked at her. "I might lick a little, too."

She gave him a flirty grin. "I'm not opposed to that, either."

Tripp chuckled before taking a drink of his whisky, then grabbed her hand, his thumb caressing across her knuckles. "So, there's something I want to ask you."

He suddenly sounded so serious, and she gave him her full attention. "Okay."

"Remember when I told you that I plant a rose bush every year in my parents' back yard to honor my sister Whitney's passing?"

She nodded, unable to forget such a touching idea and tribute to his deceased twin. "Yes. I believe you mentioned that this year will be the twentieth anniversary of her passing."

"It is," he said, and smiled. "The date is a few weeks away, on a Sunday. We always do a family get together on that day to celebrate Whitney's life, along with dinner. I'd like you to be there, too."

His invitation took her by surprise and was the last thing she expected when she wasn't a part of his family. "That's very personal for you, your parents, and your siblings."

"I know." He still held her hand, his green eyes locked on hers. "Let me rephrase what I just said. It's a special day and I *want* you there because you're important to me."

Oh, wow. Her throat tightened and his heartfelt words softened something inside of her. As much as she wasn't sure she wanted to be involved in intimate family traditions considering she and Tripp weren't a real couple, she was truly honored that he wanted to include her.

To her surprise, she couldn't deny wanting to be there for him on such a momentous occasion *as a friend.* Because if nothing else, that's what they were, weren't they? That last thought made her stomach clench with regret, despite her being the one to set the parameters of this relationship.

Doing her best to ignore those unexpected feelings, she gave him a sincere smile. "Yes, of course, I'd love to be there."

He looked relieved ... and happy. "It'll also give my family a chance to meet you and get to know you, which is important since we'll be having a baby together. You'll be part of the family, too, no matter how we choose to raise our child together."

She swallowed hard, knowing she ought to be grateful that he wasn't putting any pressure or expectations on her to be anything more than his baby mama, just as she'd insisted, but she couldn't deny wishing they were more. That her past, her fears, and her need to be independent didn't clash with old feelings for Tripp and the desire she'd always had to be part of a traditional family like the one she'd grown up in.

Their appetizers arrived, and once the server was gone she found herself asking the curious question buzzing around in her mind. "When was the last time you took someone home to meet your family?"

"About two years ago," he replied, before taking a bite of the Wagyu beef tartar they were sharing.

Skye ate a piece of seared eggplant, dying to know who this mystery woman was. Clearly, she'd been someone he'd deemed important enough to introduce to his family, but they were no longer together. "Care to elaborate?" she asked, more casually than she felt.

He shrugged, as if the woman was inconsequential. Skye selfishly wanted to believe that, but the reality was that she and Tripp had been apart for over five years. Of course he'd dated other people and probably even had a long term relationship during that time. Considering she'd been married, she had no right to feel jealous.

"Her name was Julia," he said, settling back in the booth beside her as he lifted his whisky to his lips for a drink. "She was a pharmaceutical rep I met at a conference. We dated for almost a year and a half."

That bit of information felt like a stab to the heart, no matter what she'd just tried to tell herself and she quickly glanced away before he could catch the envy she was certain was written all over her expression.

He stretched an arm across the back of the booth, his fingers sliding beneath her hair and his warm hand cupping the back of her neck. His touch was gentle and intimate and soothed the chaotic sensation in her stomach.

"You have nothing to feel jealous about, Skye," he murmured, clearly having glimpsed the painful emotions on her face. "She wasn't you."

She eased out a breath and met his sincere gaze, needing to know more. "A year and a half is a long time to be with someone. Why did you break up?"

He paused for a moment as if considering his words before speaking again. "Julia and I were compatible in a lot of ways. I wouldn't have stayed with her that long if we weren't. Things with her were . . . comfortable, and easy, and convenient. I honestly thought that maybe we'd get married and have a family, since I was finally in a position to make that kind of commitment to someone."

He laughed and shook his head. "But when I brought up the idea of getting married, she and I weren't even remotely on the same page. Her job and career were first and foremost to her, and she had no desire to tie herself to a husband and kids. So, she ended things." A wry smile twisted his lips. "I guess she did to me what I realize now I did to you. Except I didn't have strong feelings for her. At all."

Skye's eyes widened in shock, and because she didn't know what to say, she uttered a quiet, "Wow."

He lifted his shoulder. "She did the right thing by breaking things off, because the one thing I know now is that I would have been settling, because she wasn't the woman I truly wanted." He paused, then said, "You've always been the one, Skye, but I thought you were married and I'd lost my chance."

He gently stroked the back of his hand along her cheek, and she shivered at the raw emotion in his eyes as they remained focused on hers.

You've always been the one, Skye. She could feel the locks around her heart cracking open, wanting what he was offering so badly. His words were everything she'd wanted to hear all those years ago, but so much had changed in that time. Mostly, her.

As much as she still deeply cared for him, she'd come to rely on her independence and autonomy. After everything she'd endured with Jack, the last thing she wanted was to depend on any man again. For anything.

She didn't want to lose herself in Tripp, and that was her greatest fear. She'd worked so hard to carve out a new life for herself, one that, for the most part, made her happy and fulfilled. But those awful times with Jack had scarred her, the flashbacks always hovering, and while she was willing to let Tripp be a parental figure to their child, that vulnerable part of her wasn't prepared to give up the new and safe life she'd built for herself.

"Skye?"

The harsh sound of someone saying her name jolted Skye out of her troubling thoughts, and she jerked her attention from Tripp to the man standing by their table. Not just any man, either, but her brother, Spencer, whose fierce, protective gaze was narrowed on Tripp in an almost comically feral way.

"Spencer!" she said, her tone high pitched thanks to her shock at seeing him in the same hotel. He was the last person she thought she'd run into over the weekend. "What are you doing here?"

"I'm waiting for my date, who is running late," he said in a terse tone, his hands braced on his hips.

Skye was certain if they were meeting at a swanky hotel then it had to be one of Spencer's hookups.

"What are _you_ doing here?" he volleyed back.

And who the fuck is the guy you're with? She could read the harsh question in his eyes and knew that Spencer was in overprotective big brother mode—especially since she hadn't dated anyone since Jack. So she gave him a pass on his brusque attitude.

"I'm on a date, as well," she said calmly, then made the introductions. "This is Tripp Daniels. Tripp, this is my brother, Spencer."

Tripp finally pulled away the hand that had been resting on her shoulder and turned toward her brother with an amicable smile. "It's nice to meet you," he said and extended his hand to shake.

Spencer clasped Tripp's hand so tight that the veins in his forearms nearly stood out, but Tripp's grip was equally firm.

"I'd say the same, but I have no idea who the hell you are," her brother said, holding nothing back.

"Spencer!" While a part of Skye understood her brother's extreme reaction, the other part was horrified at his disrespectful behavior.

Spencer released Tripp's hand and shifted his gaze to her, an accusatory look in his eyes. "I just saw you a few days ago at the gym for kickboxing. You couldn't at least have mentioned that you had a date with some stranger?"

She winced, because her brother was right. Out of everyone in her family, he'd been the one to take care of her after Jack's abuse. He'd picked her up the day after that assault, he'd seen her at her absolute lowest, and she knew a part of him carried guilt for not stepping in sooner. He'd also spent the past two years helping to rebuild her self-esteem, and her physical strength.

But, he'd also wrapped her up in a bubble, trying to

keep her safe, to the point of being a helicopter sibling. The surprise of finding out she was dating someone had clearly been triggering for him, even though it was bound to happen at some point.

God, this was not how she wanted her brother to meet Tripp for the first time. She thought she'd have the opportunity to build up Tripp's character before she introduced them, or announced that he'd fathered her child when the time came.

"Can you please sit down so we can have a civilized conversation—and so the entire lounge isn't staring at us?" she asked him.

To her relief, Spencer slid into the booth opposite them and set his cellphone on the table. Unfortunately, the furrow between his brows lingered as he glared at Tripp, who remained impressively composed and was letting her handle the situation. Thank God. She didn't need the two men in her life posturing over her.

"Tripp isn't a stranger," she told her brother once he was settled. "I've known him since before Jack. Do you remember me telling you about the guy I was dating back then, the one who was in med school? Tripp is that guy."

The recollection flashed across Spencer's handsome features. She thought that the fact that Tripp was someone she already knew would soften her brother's reaction, or gain Tripp a few points, but that knowledge seemed to irritate Spencer even more.

"Wait a minute," Spencer said, his entire body stiffening. "You mean to tell me this is the guy who ended things because he had commitment issues?"

She almost snorted a laugh, considering her brother was the king of playing the field and avoiding long term relationships.

Up to this point, Tripp had remained quiet, taking her brother's jabs in stride. But now, he opened his mouth to reply to Spencer's scathing remark. Skye put a hand on his thigh beneath the table to stop him. Tripp held back his reply and with a quick glance at him, she saw the annoyance in his narrowed eyes.

She needed to handle her brother and despite Tripp's growing irritation, she knew he would be understanding. "Would you mind giving me and Spencer a few minutes alone?"

He gave her a curt nod. "Sure thing," he said, and slid out of the booth before walking out of the lounge . . . Spencer's scowl following him all the way.

As soon as Tripp left, she reached across the table and clasped her brother's hands in hers so she had his complete attention. "I know you mean well and your intentions are good when it comes to protecting me because of everything that happened with Jack, but you have to know that I won't *ever* put myself in that kind of situation again. Trust me, I'm a much better judge of character now than I was before marrying Jack."

She felt the tension ease from Spencer's hands, and his stiff shoulders relaxed. "I can't help but worry about you." He ran a hand through his hair, his frustration obvious.

"I know," she said, and smiled. "You've been an amazing big brother these past few years. More than I can ever repay. And you're right. I should have told you that I was going out on a date with someone when I saw you last, but I was afraid of you acting just like this if I told you about Tripp. And I didn't want to have an argument. I'm sorry that you were blind-sided."

"It's okay." Spencer shifted in his seat. "I was an ass to your … friend."

"Yes, you were," she said with a shake of her head and an understanding grin.

The situation diffused, this was the point where she should have mentioned the drawing she'd received from Jack in the mail yesterday but she'd just gotten Spencer's ruffled feathers settled. Hearing about Jack's *reappearance* in her life would ramp him right back into over-bearing mode. Without a direct physical threat, there was nothing anyone could do about the fact that Jack had sent her a letter that was most likely his way of trying to scare her and manipulate her emotions. Neither of which she would allow.

Then, there was her current secret. She was trying to conceive a baby with Tripp, instead of going the insemination route as Spencer and the rest of her family believed. This wasn't the time or the place to explain her arrangement with Tripp or have any kind of embarrassing conversation with her brother. When and if she turned up pregnant, then she'd address the new status quo.

"I just don't want this Tripp guy to take advantage of you," Spencer said, huffing out a deep breath. "And most importantly, I don't want you to end up with another asshole like Jack."

She gave him a smile. "I appreciate your concern, I really do, but that's the last thing you have to worry about with Tripp." That much she knew without a doubt.

"Even though he broke your heart in the past?" Spencer pointed out.

She nodded. "Yes. We were both young and the timing between us was all wrong." She could look back with a clear mind and admit that now, even if the result had been her meeting and marrying Jack.

Her brother tipped his head to the side, not completely convinced. "And now it's not?"

"And now . . . well, we're reconnecting," she said carefully. "And I'd like you to give Tripp a fair chance and get to know him because he really is a good, upstanding guy."

Spencer hesitated a moment, then spoke. "Okay." The look in his eyes finally softened, as if he truly realized how important this was to her—even if he didn't know why. "For you, I will."

She exhaled a breath, her own stress level over the situation alleviated. "Thank you, Spence."

By the time Tripp returned to the table, her brother was noticeably calmer.

Spencer ran his fingers through his dark blond hair and shifted uncomfortably in his seat before addressing Tripp. "Hey, man."

Skye held her breath as she waited to see what her brother might say.

"I'm really sorry that I was a jerk when I came to the table earlier. It was a gut reaction more than anything," Spencer said, manning up, and making her proud of him.

"I understand," Tripp said, his tone sincere. "I'm just glad Skye has a brother who cares so much and looks out for her."

"*Always*," Spencer replied, and Skye tried not to roll her eyes at the subtle warning in her brother's tone, as if he was silently making sure that Tripp knew he'd be answering to *him* if he hurt Skye in any way.

The cellphone that Spencer had placed on the table buzzed, and he checked whatever message had just come through. "My date just got here and we're heading to the restaurant for dinner. You two want to join us?" he asked, clearly extending an olive branch.

She appreciated the offer, but the last thing she wanted to do was sit through a long meal with Spencer and whatever woman he was hooking up with, making small talk. No, she'd rather head back to the penthouse and spend the rest of the evening alone with Tripp.

"Thank you, but we have other plans," she said, then realizing how that sounded, she added quickly, "Have a nice evening with your lady friend."

Spencer stood up to leave, and this time when the men shook hands, they did so with mutual respect, like civilized gentlemen.

Once her brother was gone, Skye leaned back in her seat and exhaled a long breath, feeling as though she'd just been put through the wringer. "Well, *that* was fun," she said, her tone wry.

Tripp groaned as he withdrew cash from his wallet to pay their bill, along with a generous tip. "Definitely *not* my idea of a good time, getting lambasted by my girl's brother."

She arched a playful brow at him, beyond ready to lighten things up after that heavy conversation with Spencer. "Then tell me, what *is* your idea of a good time?" she asked in a seductive tone.

Tripp turned fully toward her, his body shielding her from anyone looking their way as he placed a hand on her knee beneath the table. Leaning closer, he put his mouth to her ear as he slowly slid his hot palm up her thigh. "How about you, naked, and moaning my name while I do dirty, filthy things to this delectable pussy, which, as I recall, I promised to lick and eat?"

Need instantly clamored inside of her, and she parted her legs as he skimmed those wicked fingers higher, until he encountered bare, damp flesh.

"*Fuck.*" He growled against her neck at the discovery. "I had no idea you weren't wearing any panties tonight."

"Surprise," she said, her voice soft and breathless as he fingered her, her arousal ramping up at the possibility of them getting caught in such a compromising position. "Just providing easy access, as you'd requested."

"Such a naughty, dirty girl," he said on a low growl.

She gasped as he pushed two fingers deep, sweeping his thumb across her clit and lighting up sensitive nerve endings.

"*That* order was for when we were in the suite, not out in public, but I'm not going to deny this is so damn hot. Though, I ought to punish you for being so bad by making you come right here and now," he said, as he pumped those thick digits in and out of her, and it took all her effort not to squirm or grind down on his hand for more friction.

She whimpered, for his ears only, as with every stroke she melted, her body turning into a molten puddle of lust and need.

He lifted his head and she glanced at him with desperation, unsure if he was going to follow through on his threat to make her come in the dimly lit lounge. She was torn between being appalled at the idea, and wanting him to do just that.

He smirked, his eyes dark and hot as he withdrew his fingers and lifted them to his lips, boldly sucking the taste of her off his fingers. "Honey and apricots," he murmured wickedly. "Who the fuck needs dessert when I have you to enjoy? Ready to head upstairs so I can fuck you so hard and deep you'll feel my cock all the way up to your throat?"

That wasn't possible, of course, but she shuddered at his filthy words, trying to remain composed when all she wanted was for him to manhandle her, to make her scream in ecstasy, again and again, and make her completely his.

"Yes, please," she whispered.

Once the words were spoken, they couldn't get back to their room fast enough. They had one night left together, and she wanted to make the most of it.

As SOON AS they walked into the suite, Tripp grabbed Skye and kissed her, his mouth hot and hungry on hers. Their hands frantically tore at each other's clothes to remove them, leaving a trail of garments in their wake as he maneuvered them toward the bedroom, both of them desperate to feel skin on skin.

Pure lust and fire erupted between them, as it always did, and Tripp picked up Skye and tossed her onto the bed. She landed with a squeak of surprise, her breasts bouncing enticingly, then moaned when he shoved her legs indecently wide apart and wasted no time dragging his tongue through the sweetest, softest pussy he'd ever had the pleasure of devouring.

She rocked her hips up against his mouth, silently, wantonly begging, and as soon as he latched onto her clit and sucked hard, followed by plunging two fingers deep inside her core, she whimpered and gripped the comforter to hang on as he sent her soaring. Her entire body shook, her back arched, and her thighs tightened against his head as she rode out her pleasure.

The first orgasm was quick and dirty, just as he'd intended to take off the initial edge and make her slick and hot and wet enough to accept everything he planned to give her. He wanted to be as deep as he could possibly get inside her, until she had no idea where she ended and he began.

There was nothing soft, or gentle, or slow about his need for this woman who owned his heart. Tonight, he wanted her to feel him everywhere as he imprinted his scent on her skin, filled her full of his cock, and ruined her for any other man but him. Because despite all her reservations and fears, she was his. She would *always* be his.

He gave her minimal time to recover from her orgasm before he flipped her over onto her stomach, then grabbed her hips and raised her ass high so he could fuck her from behind. Her upper body was still lax, her cheek pressed against the mattress, so trusting as he ran his hands over her smooth flesh before smacking her ass, then notching the thick head of his cock between her legs, just enough to tease.

She moaned sweetly at the pressure and promise of his dick, trying to push back onto his shaft even more. "Tripp, please . . ."

"Please *what*, baby girl?" he murmured, admiring the long, gorgeous line of her bare back as he sank in another inch.

A frustrated sound escaped her. "I need you inside me, as hard and deep as you can get. *Please.*"

Grabbing her waist and holding her steady, he

slammed to the hilt inside her, making her cry out from the force of his thrust. He didn't stop there, didn't give her time to catch her breath as he reared back and continued pounding into her, groaning at the feel of her tight pussy sucking him in deeper each time.

He slid a hand along her hip and around to her belly, then down between her legs, where they were joined. Still grinding into her from behind, he rubbed her clit just how he knew she liked it, working her into a delirious frenzy of need and feeling her tense up as he drove her higher, then pushed her over the precipice.

She came a second time around his cock with a soft, keening cry, her inner walls squeezing his length and triggering his own intense release.

With deep, guttural grunts, he poured everything he had into her, desperately wanting to give her the one thing they both desired the most. A baby. *Their* baby. Because no matter how guarded she remained with him, a child would ensure that he was always a part of her life.

And that knowledge, at least, gave him hope that he could eventually win back her heart.

Chapter Twelve

SKYE CHEWED ON her thumbnail as she paced anxiously in her living room, waiting impatiently for Tripp to arrive. She wasn't going to take this pregnancy test without him, because good or bad, he deserved to find out when she did if they'd created a baby together.

A little over three weeks had passed since their weekend at The Meridian, and since Skye wasn't one of those women who had a regular menstrual cycle, except for when she'd been on the pill, it made detecting a missed period difficult. The last thing she wanted to do was jump the gun and take a test and end up with a false positive. After consulting with a few online fertility clinics, she'd learned that the best chance for accurate results was three weeks after sex and/or ovulation.

So, here she was, excited and nervous and trying not to overthink the increasing changes she'd been feeling in her body the past few days, so she wouldn't be disappointed if the test was negative. She wanted to be pregnant so badly, but the increasing tenderness in her breasts could have been normal pre-menstrual symptoms.

But it was the random waves of nausea she'd been experiencing, along with headaches and fatigue that Lauren had pointed out, that finally convinced Skye to take a home pregnancy test. So, before leaving work for the day, a Friday, she'd texted Tripp to let him know she was going to stop at the drugstore and pick up a few tests on the way home, and he promised her he'd be there as soon as he finished up the tonsillectomy he had scheduled for that afternoon.

That low level sense of discomfort swirled in her stomach—nerves, excitement or pregnancy hormones, she really had no idea—and she headed into the kitchen to grab a can of ginger ale that she could sip on while she waited for Tripp to arrive.

Since their weekend at The Meridian, he'd respected her *no sex rule* outside of trying to make a baby, but he'd somehow integrated himself into her life in a way that felt like he belonged there. Not just nightly FaceTiming, but quick lunches when their schedules aligned during the day, and stopping by in the evenings just to bring her dinner and hang out and watch a show.

She could honestly say that she wasn't mad about having that friendship in her life, even if at times it felt like so much more. In fact, she'd grown used to picking up her phone and texting Tripp throughout the day, and anticipated seeing him one way or another at night, even if she found it increasingly difficult to keep her hands to herself when everything in her ached to feel him deep inside her again.

But she was determined not to blur the lines between them. She loved spending time with him, and had to fight off an increasing sense of loneliness when they parted ways, telling herself that her apartment wouldn't be quiet forever, not when she had a baby filling the space with cries of hunger, happy gurgles, and when he or she was older, sweet laughter. Which made her think of Tripp, and how he deserved to experience those milestone moments, too ... or maybe it was *she* that wanted to experience those moments with *him*.

Sighing, she rubbed her fingers along her forehead, her emotions a jumble of confusion when it came to her feelings for the man who'd made himself a part of her life. Wanting him there, yet ... scared of letting her guard down and letting him in completely and trusting him with her heart a second time. Not that she believed Tripp would hurt her or manipulate her in the way Jack had but she just couldn't get over that final hump. Her fear of commitment and relying on anyone, so completely.

A brisk knock at her door jarred Skye out of her thoughts and reminded her of why Tripp was here. To find out if they'd conceived a baby.

But when she opened the door and saw him standing on the other side, it wasn't excitement or anticipation she saw on his face for what might lay ahead, but the kind of worry and concern that sent her stomach spiraling into another wave of nausea.

✧   ✧   ✧

TRIPP PULLED OUT of the hospital parking lot after his late afternoon emergency tonsillectomy on a sweet six-year-old little girl, and headed to Skye's where she was waiting for him to arrive before taking a pregnancy test. He was more excited than nervous to find out if he'd gotten the job done, because despite her determination to keep them as *just friends*, a baby would change everything and bond them more intimately.

As he drove toward Skye's place in Brooklyn, he glanced in his rear view mirror and frowned at the black sedan following way too fucking close behind him. A car he identified as the same one he'd seen tailing him two other times this past week—each time, the sedan trailed him from his office to right before he reached Skye's building. At that point, the vehicle would turn down a side street and disappear.

Tripp's instincts told him this wasn't a coincidence. He didn't recognize the dark haired man in the driver's seat wearing tinted sunglasses hiding his features. But this was becoming a frequent occurrence whenever he drove to Skye's and Tripp was both wary and concerned because who else could it be but Skye's ex?

Still, he had no evidence it was Jack, and he couldn't get a good enough look at the man in the car to identify him, even if he found a photo of her ex on social media to compare. There had been no other contact since that drawing but that didn't mean the douchebag wasn't skulking around, waiting for an opportunity to approach Skye when she was alone. And that was not something Tripp wanted to consider.

When he reached Skye's quiet neighborhood on a residential street, the asshole behind him shot around Tripp's car, then cut him off, stopping abruptly and forcing Tripp to white-knuckle his steering wheel as he slammed on his brakes. Otherwise he'd have rear-ended the sedan and crushed his front end.

"Fucking asshole!" Tripp yelled, unimpressed by the way the guy revved his engine, trying to exert some big dick energy when he probably had nothing more than a micro-penis. What the hell was this jerk's problem?

Done with his antics, Tripp grabbed his phone and snapped a photo the other car's license plate, seconds before the sedan peeled away, burning rubber and running through a nearby stop sign like a jackass. He obviously didn't give a shit if he hurt someone else in his quest to intimidate Tripp, which wasn't happening.

Jesus fucking Christ. He exhaled slow and deep, his entire body vibrating with rage, because if the man in the other car *was* Skye's ex, the thought of her being harassed and terrorized in the same way made Tripp's blood run cold.

He had to prove this asshole was Jack and at least now Tripp had a license plate number. According to his brother, Beck, his friend, Zach Dare, not only owned The Back Door Bar, but he had mad hacking skills and connections inside the police department. No doubt, Zach could get him the information he needed to find out who this guy was, and Tripp sent off a quick text to Beck asking for the other man's phone number to contact him.

By the time Tripp made it up to Skye's apartment, the worst of his adrenaline rush had worn off, but he couldn't completely extinguish the concern twisting through him.

"What's wrong?" she asked. Obviously, she'd taken one look at his face, and sensed something was off. She pressed a hand to her stomach as she opened the door wider to let him in. "Is everything okay?"

He intended to tell her what had just happened—no way was he keeping something so important from her—but he also knew how anxious she was to find out if she was pregnant. The last thing he wanted to do was put a major damper on their exciting moment by bringing up her ex, and the possibility of him being in the city.

"Everything's fine," he assured her, summoning a smile.

He'd already been frustrated that they lived in separate places but now he dreaded leaving because he wanted to protect her since his gut told him Jack *was* in town. Decision made. Tripp wasn't leaving Skye alone until he had more details on the driver of that sedan, and he was certain that announcement would upset her and cause friction between him and the newly independent Skye. Not that he cared if she put up a fuss, because he wasn't taking any chances with her welfare.

"So, are you ready to find out if you're pregnant?" he asked to distract her, while noticing that her complexion looked softer, and smoother recently. Not necessarily a glow, but beautiful, nonetheless.

She bit her bottom lip and nodded. "Weirdly nervous, but hopeful."

"Me, too." He leaned in and placed a chaste kiss on her forehead. "Don't be discouraged if it doesn't happen this first time," he said, not wanting to defuse that optimistic look in her eyes, but also needing to be realistic about the possibilities.

She nodded, and for now he forced himself to be present in the moment, because if she *was* pregnant, this should be a memorable occasion for them both, not marked by any worries or mention of her ex. That would come soon enough.

"The test is in the bathroom," she said, exhaling a deep, fortifying breath. "So, I'll go pee on the stick and see what happens."

He accompanied her into the bedroom and sat down on her bed while she went to the bathroom. After a few minutes, she returned, holding the test strip behind her back.

"I didn't want to look and see the results without you." Her eyes twinkled with a mix of excitement and apprehension.

All he could think of was how grateful he was that she'd gone out of her way to include him in the smallest parts of the journey.

She waited for him to stand up and join her before

revealing the plastic device for them both to look at together.

Two bright pink lines stood out, and Skye gasped in shock. "Oh, my God. It's positive," she said, laughing happily as her eyes shimmered with tears. "We did it. I'm *pregnant*." She threw her arms around his neck and hugged him, and he pulled her tight and close, absorbing her ecstatic response and unfiltered joy.

He, too, was filled with wonder and awe that they'd created a baby together. Shock and disbelief that he was going to be a father. But mixed in with all that happiness was a fierce, overwhelming protectiveness toward Skye and their unborn child. Right after came the thought that he would lay down his own life to ensure their wellbeing.

Despite them not being married, she and the baby were his to care for. His to keep safe, because mother and child were explicably intertwined in his heart—even if Skye didn't want them to be. And he resented the fact that *his* moment was tempered by her fucking ex-husband and he hated that he was going to have to burst Skye's jubilant bubble, too.

She finally released him from her hug, a wide, brilliant smile on her flushed face. "I know we're seeing your family this weekend for Whitney's memorial, but I don't want to say anything until we've had a chance to visit a doctor and confirm everything is good."

"I'm fine with that," he said, and noticed how she absently rubbed a hand along her black yoga pants, over her still flat stomach. Suddenly, a slight frown creased her brow.

"What's wrong?" he asked.

"I've been queasy throughout the day and wasn't sure if it was pregnancy related," she admitted, and wrinkled her nose in that adorable way of hers. "But I know I should eat something, too."

He headed into her small kitchen area and opened up the refrigerator, scanning the contents. "How about I make you something that will be easy on your stomach, like some scrambled eggs and toast and some fruit?"

"Yeah, that sounds good, thanks."

While she sat at the table, he whipped up a plate of food for each of them, essentially making breakfast for dinner. After they finished eating, she leaned back in her chair, smiling and looking so happy and content, her hand once again over her abdomen, as if she was already protecting the little life growing inside. But Tripp knew he couldn't put off the inevitable any longer. He had to tell her the truth.

"Skye . . . something happened today. Right before I arrived at your apartment," he said, meeting and holding her gaze. "I didn't want to take away from the big moment, but now it can't wait."

That blissful smile she'd been wearing all through their meal fell away, replaced by a wary look in her eyes. "Okay."

He exhaled a breath and explained about the sedan, and the fact that this had been the third time he'd been followed to her place by the same vehicle and sunglasses wearing driver. And how today things had escalated to aggressive and threatening.

She leaned forward and met his gaze, remaining silent so he couldn't know what she was thinking. If she'd made the same connection he had.

"I think it's your ex behind the stalking," he said, because the actions were exactly that—harassment and intimidation, meant to make Tripp feel threatened. No doubt, Jack resented Tripp's relationship with the woman he still considered his.

"But Jack lives and works in Boston," Skye said, clearly trying to explain away Tripp's theory because to believe it would mean her worst fears were coming true. "Why would he bother to harass you of all people?" she asked.

Because despite everything, a psychopath like your ex still wants you for himself.

But Tripp wouldn't say it that way. Reaching out, he clasped Skye's free hand, seeking both the connection he needed and to reassure her.

The truth was Jack's attempt to frighten Tripp had worked. Not because he was concerned for himself, but her ex's sole interest would be in Skye. To get to her, he needed Tripp out of the way before making a move on a defenseless woman. What the asshole didn't know or take into consideration was the fact that Tripp wouldn't be run off.

Even though his thoughts were all speculation, Tripp trusted his gut.

"Boston isn't that far," he reminded her, easing into the hard truths. "If it is Jack, he's probably trying to warn me away from you."

She yanked her hand free. "But—"

"Listen to me," he said, his voice more serious than it had ever been. "You have no idea what he's done in the past year since you moved to New York. Where he's working or even where he's living."

"No, but him leaving his life? His home? It all seems . . . extreme, even for him. Especially a long year after our divorce has been finalized," she said, still trying to be logical because logic would keep her safe. "It could have just been someone with road rage tendencies."

"The same guy, the same car, three separate times? I doubt it." He needed her to believe his theory if he was going to keep her safe. "It's one man. And if Jack has discovered that you and I are involved, then he's trying to send a threatening message."

Her lips pursed, and her chin lifted obstinately. "I still have a protective order against him from before our divorce. It's valid across state lines."

As if a piece of paper would be enough to dissuade a determined, narcissistic man like Jack from taking what he considered his. Tripp understood Skye's reasons for fighting him but she wouldn't win. He'd rather be wrong than risk her and their unborn child in any way.

"If we assume he cares about the protective order, that's even more of a reason for him to focus on me first and not approach you. . . yet."

She rubbed her hands along her thighs, her face pinched with anger, and he watched her struggle with the possibility of her ex turning her life upside down again. "Even if it's him, I refuse to let Jack rule my life again. I can't live in fear any more, and I can take care of myself. Spencer made sure of that by teaching me self-defense."

Tripp shook his head, both proud of and frustrated by her attitude.

His decision would not sit well with her and he braced for her anger. "I respect that but I'm not taking any chances with you, or our baby," he said, his tone firm. Just the thought of Skye or the child inside her being hurt incited his rage and made him feel violent.

"What are you saying?" she asked warily, both fists clenched.

"First, I have a picture of the license plate number. I'm going to get in touch with Zach Dare and see if he can find out who the vehicle is registered to. I can't do a thing without proof that it's Jack. Based on the plates, the car wasn't a rental, which gives us a shot of nailing him. But until I know for sure, I'm going to make certain that you're safe. Which means I'll be staying with you for the foreseeable future."

She stiffened, her frustration palpable. "So, I don't get a choice in the matter?"

"Of course you have a choice," he said, crossing his arms over his chest. "My place or yours."

His reply didn't amuse her even a little. She looked

upset, conflicted, then finally, resigned.

"Fine," she said, her tone still defiant, which didn't surprise Tripp in the least. "You can stay here." She rose from her seat and took her plate to the sink. "On the couch," she informed him, before stalking out of the room.

Chapter Thirteen

SKYE WOKE UP on Sunday morning in bed alone—while Tripp had spent his second night on the couch. Guilt tightened her chest as she ran her hand over the cool sheets beside hers, feeling contrite for her behavior toward him when he only had good intentions when it came to protecting her.

She'd had more than enough time to indulge her sulky mood over his insistence that he stay with her until he received the information about the driver of the black sedan. She wanted to believe it was all a coincidence, but truth be told, she was feeling that old anxiety swirling inside her at the possibility that Jack was reinserting himself back into her life, and she hated that her ex still had that much power over her emotions.

She'd given herself a full day to embrace her annoyance over the entire situation, which had probably been exacerbated by her pregnancy hormones—or that's the excuse she was telling herself anyway. Yesterday, she'd gone about her normal Saturday routine, although with Tripp glued to her side as she ran her errands and grocery shopped for the week. She even strolled through a small bookstore for a new novel and sat outdoors at her favorite café for lunch while he ate a burger and kept a watchful eye on everything going on around them.

But even knowing that Tripp was right there beside her the entire day, Skye had been hyper aware of everyone around her—cars that might be following them and anything else out of her normal routine that triggered old memories of Jack. And by the time they'd returned back to her apartment, she felt stressed-out and her nerves were stretched thin, which put her in a snappy mood.

While most men would have probably called her on her irritable attitude, Tripp had taken it all in stride, remaining calm and unaffected by her mood swings, which couldn't have been an easy feat. When they were in her apartment, he'd given her space, even when she'd told him after dinner that she wanted to read a book in bed. Alone. And then had sequestered herself in her bedroom for the rest of the evening.

If she'd been trying to make a point to herself that she preferred being on her own and didn't need a man in her life, her plan had backfired. She hadn't been able to concentrate on the book she'd bought, and instead wished that she was out in the living room with Tripp, watching a movie with him. And sleeping alone in her bed when he was just one room away had been pure torture when she could have been wrapped up in his strong arms and cuddled against his chest.

The truth was . . . she *liked* having Tripp at her

place. And the weekend would have been so much more pleasant if she hadn't been so sulky. It was time to snap out of her funk. She owed Tripp an apology. He deserved to have a nice day at his parent's for Whitney's memorial, and the last thing she wanted was any of her lingering insecurities ruining this special occasion for him.

Getting out of bed, she went into the bathroom to take care of business and brushed her teeth. Still wearing her pajamas—a cotton tank top and shorts—she padded out to the living room in search of Tripp. The blanket she'd given him was folded neatly and stacked on the pillow at the end of the couch, indicating he'd been up for a while.

She found him in the kitchen—shirtless and wearing just a pair of jeans, making a cup of coffee. The rich, fragrant scent, which normally made her crave caffeine, caused her unpredictable stomach to lurch, but not enough to send her running for the toilet, thank goodness.

She groaned in disappointment that she wasn't going to be able to enjoy a cup. Her waves of nausea were random, and so far she couldn't pinpoint what set off the queasy feeling, but thankfully she'd been able to maintain her composure.

He turned around at the sound she'd made, and while she blatantly admired his bare chest and sexy, sleep tousled hair, his dark green eyes dipped down to her breasts, which felt heavier and more sensitive this morning. Beneath her tank top, her nipples tightened, and her clit pulsed, reminding her what she was missing out on by imposing her no sex rule.

Tripp gradually lifted his gaze back to hers, his own desire for her evident on his face. "Morning," he said in a neutral tone, clearly trying to be polite because he had no idea what kind of attitude he was going to get from her today. Not that she blamed him.

"Morning." She stepped toward him, then stopped, unsure of what kind of reception *she* was going to get, either, after her prickly disposition yesterday. "I owe you an apology. I'm sorry I've been so moody since Friday night."

A small smile curved his sensual lips. He closed the distance between them and wrapped his arms around her, pulling her in for a gentle, caring and very unexpected hug. Burrowing against his bare chest, she closed her eyes and absorbed his warmth, his strength, and the intoxicating male scent of his skin.

But mostly, she reveled in his easy forgiveness and unconditional acceptance. He didn't hold a grudge for her day of crises as her ex would have, or withhold his affection, or even make her feel bad for how she'd handled things. He just accepted her—the good, the bad, and the bitchy.

"I know this isn't easy on you, Skye," he murmured, stroking his fingers along the back of her head, still holding her close. "But you have to know that I will *always* protect you, even when you don't want me to. When it comes to you, it's instinctive and not something I can turn off or ignore. And I'll do the same for our child. I will always be here for you."

His heartfelt words were like a balm to her soul, a safe haven, even. "I know," she whispered, believing every word he said. "I appreciate the man you are, more than I can ever say." And that was true, as well.

He lifted his head and stared down at her, saying nothing, but the tender, caring look in his eyes said everything. Her lips parted, her heart beating slow and steady and sure in her chest, and when he didn't make the first move, she did.

Lifting up on her toes, she lightly pressed her mouth to his and kissed him—the kind that was soft and sweet and intimate, without any expectation of more. It spoke of kindness, appreciation, and reverence, and the words *I love you* rose up into her throat, aching to be let loose, but she managed to hold them back.

The sentiment came so naturally, in a way that told Skye that despite her best efforts, she'd fallen in love with Tripp all over again. Truthfully, she wasn't shocked or surprised considering what a good man he was, but she wasn't sure what to do with this newfound knowledge and her feelings for him. Or those insecurities and fears that were still present.

She ended the chaste kiss and stepped back, and he let her go, as if sensing she needed that space—that's how in tune to her he always was. He didn't say anything about that heartfelt kiss, nor did he ask why she'd instigated it or what it meant.

Instead, he slid his hand beneath the hem of her

tank top and gently pressed his palm to her still flat belly, as if he was touching the most precious thing in the universe. Her breath caught at the poignancy of the moment. Their baby was nothing more than a little bean so there was nothing for either of them to feel right now, except for the connection and intimacy of having created a child together.

And that seemed to be enough for him. For her, too.

He met her gaze and smiled, and she didn't miss the sexy, possessive glimmer in his eyes. "How are you and our little sprout doing this morning?"

The nickname was silly, but she loved it. "We're okay."

"Good." He caressed her belly one last time before letting his hand fall away. "Let's figure out what we're going to feed you two."

She watched him head to the refrigerator to find things to make for breakfast and she knew, despite all the crazy uncertainty of the weekend tainted by worries of Jack interfering in her life once again, she and Tripp were going to have a special day at his parents later that afternoon.

✧ ✧ ✧

TRIPP PARKED HIS car outside of his parents' house and turned off the engine, watching as Skye stared out the passenger window at their front yard and fidgeted restlessly in her seat. She'd spent the past half hour drive battling her nerves—smoothing a hand along the skirt of her dress, slowly inhaling and exhaling, and absently biting her lower lip.

"Ready to head inside?" he asked, giving his rear view mirror one last glance, just to make sure they hadn't been followed by a black sedan. He wasn't being paranoid, just extremely cautious. "Looks like everyone else is already here." Drew and Beck's vehicles were parked in the driveway.

She finally looked at him, a glimmer of curiosity in her gaze. "What are you going to tell them, about us?"

He sighed. Yes, he already knew that introductions were going to be quite the dilemma. He and Skye weren't dating, and she wasn't technically his girlfriend, but she *was* pregnant with his baby. They didn't intend to make that announcement today, so for now, the friend zone it was.

"I'm going to tell them that you're a good friend, and that's all they're going to care about," he said, reaching out and stroking his fingers along her soft cheek. "I promise that they aren't going to read into the situation, or interrogate you, or make you feel uncomfortable. My parents and brothers are friendly, easy going kind of people. They'll welcome you because you're with me, simple as that."

Okay, that wasn't entirely true. His parents would be lovely to Skye, but his brothers . . . yeah, Beck and Drew would realize that Tripp bringing someone to Whitney's memorial was huge. He'd never shared that special day with another woman, not even Julia. So there would be speculation, but he didn't want to freak Skye out.

She nodded her head, squared her shoulders, and gave him a genuine smile. "Okay, let's do this."

They got out of the car and as soon as he met up with her by the walkway, he reached for her hand, just to offer reassurance and because it was an instinctive reaction when it came to Skye, then stopped . . . because a *friend* wouldn't have been so intimate. So, instead, he tamped down his frustration and lightly pressed his fingers to her lower back as they made their way up to the front porch.

He let himself into his parents' house and followed the sound of voices to the living room, where everyone was gathered. The first person to see him was his three year old niece, his twin's namesake, Whitney, who alerted everyone else to their presence.

"Uncle Tipp is here!" she shrieked in a boisterous voice, still unable to pronounce her "r"s, then ran over and jumped up and down in front of him, her arms raised high for him to pick her up.

Which he did, because there was no ignoring the little girl. She threw her arms around his neck and gave him a noisy kiss on his cheek. It didn't matter the reason for their family get togethers, Whitney always loved being the center of attention and spread the love and hugs between everyone equally. And truth be told, the entire family enjoyed her infectious, exuberant personality.

"Who's that?" she asked in a loud voice, pointing

to Skye, who was standing beside Tripp and smiling at the little girl.

The kid had no filter, but in all fairness she was just voicing what Tripp's parents and brothers were wondering, as well, since he could clearly see the curiosity on their faces. He'd given them no prior knowledge that he'd be bringing a plus one today.

He set Whitney back down, then made the introductions. "Everyone, this is Skye, a friend of mine," he said.

Tripp then pointed out everyone by name for Skye—his parents, Audrey and Kurt, Beck, Chloe, Drew, and . . . a pretty, blonde haired woman he hadn't formally met yet, either, but one he recognized as the woman who'd won Drew at the auction, even though it had been her sister who'd bid on him.

Everyone greeted Skye, immediately making her feel welcome, and she greeted them warmly in return.

"And this is Georgia," Drew said, sliding an arm around the blonde woman at his side who wore a shy smile, making it clear that things had worked out between them beyond his bachelor auction weekend obligation to her. "She met everyone at the family barbeque a few weeks back. The one you missed because you were on call and had an issue with a patient."

He nodded, remembering the child that had gone into respiratory distress from a severe asthma attack that day. He hadn't had a chance to talk to Drew since the auction, and he was happy to see his brother so

CARLY PHILLIPS & ERIKA WILDE

relaxed and content. Which was kind of shocking to Tripp since Drew had put any kind of relationship with a woman on the back burner in lieu of his career as an attorney. Clearly, something about Georgia had changed his mind.

"Boys, there's beer out in the cooler on the back patio," Audrey announced, shooing the men toward the slider door. "The girls and I are going to get a glass of wine and meet you out there in a few minutes."

Tripp caught Skye's gaze, silently asking her if she was going to be okay.

She gave him a sweet smile and an imperceptible nod. "I'll be fine," she assured him.

Chloe swooped in and hooked her arm through Skye's, flashing him a gregarious grin. "Don't worry, Tripp. We won't corrupt her too much."

He rolled his eyes, but appreciated his sister-in-law's kindness toward Skye. Also, he was certain that Chloe wanted to know everything about his "friendship" with her, because she'd clearly seen his interest in Skye during the charity event.

He headed outside with his father and brothers. It was a gorgeous, sunny day, perfect for planting another rose bush in Whitney's honor. A large gallon sized plastic bucket with a pruned rose bush inside sat on the deck, which Tripp had ordered and had delivered for today's memorial. There were no blooms yet, but in the spring the bush would be vibrant with deep purple hybrid roses.

Drew passed out the beers while Beck didn't waste

time mincing words.

"Friends, huh?" he asked as he twisted the top off his bottle of beer.

Tripp shrugged. "For now."

His brother smirked knowingly. "Her choice or yours, because friends do not look at friends like they want to fu—"

"Beck!" their father barked out from where he was sitting in his patio chair, cutting him off with a frown. "Skye seems like a nice girl, and there's nothing wrong with being friends."

"With benefits," Drew added with a snicker.

Despite the fact that Tripp and his siblings were all grown adults, there were times when they were together that they still acted like the brainless thirteen-year-old boys they'd once been.

"Skye isn't someone I recently met," Tripp divulged before taking a long drink of his beer. "I dated her back in Boston when I was in med school, so I've known her for a while."

"Why did you break up?" Beck asked.

Tripp absently glanced out at his parents' beautifully landscaped yard, something his father took pride in now that he was retired and in remission from cancer. "At the time, I was so overwhelmed with school and my residency, I felt like I couldn't give her the commitment she wanted."

Drew groaned in commiseration. "I just recently learned that lesson, too. I believed I couldn't have both a career and a relationship, and I would have lost

Georgia if I hadn't pulled my head out of my ass and realized she was the best thing that's ever happened to me, and that I *can* balance both."

Tripp smiled at Drew, happy for him. "Unfortunately, I had to learn the hard way, because letting Skye go back then was one of my biggest regrets. I'm just glad that I've got a second chance with her."

"Sounds . . . serious," Beck said quietly.

Tripp nodded. "It is. For me," he said, then gave them a bit more information to better understand Skye's hesitancy. "She had a bad marriage and now she's cautious and guarded, but I'm not going anywhere."

"That's what us Daniels men do," his father said, and lifted his bottle of beer toward his three sons in a salute. "We fight for the women we love."

Tripp grinned, because there was no denying he *was* in love with Skye.

"Damn straight we do," Beck said, having had his own struggles with winning over Chloe, since her brother, Linc, had been Beck's *ex*-best friend.

Their father stood up from his chair. "Drew, come and help me get some shovels and fertilizer for the new rose bush," he said, and together the duo headed toward the shed in the backyard, leaving Beck and Tripp alone for a few minutes.

"What happened with Zach?" Beck asked once it was just the two of them. "Was he able to help you out, and get the information you needed from the license plate?"

Tripp glanced inside the house to make sure the women were still in the kitchen, because this wasn't a conversation he wanted Skye to overhear. From what he could see through the glass slider, the women were still gathered around the block island, chatting away.

"Actually, he got back to me pretty quickly, which I appreciated," he said, then explained the entire situation more thoroughly to Beck, which he hadn't had time to do during their brief text exchange on Friday night. About being followed to Skye's at least three times that he knew of, and the confrontation when the asshole had turned aggressive and cut him off, and how Tripp was certain her ex-husband, Jack, was somehow involved.

"I would have bet money that the car was registered to Skye's ex, but it came back as belonging to a Doug Hammond." Tripp shook his head, disappointed at what he'd learned.

"The guy driving the car is clearly unhinged, but it's good that it's not her ex, right?" Beck asked optimistically.

Tripp's jaw clenched tight. "The thing is, I'm not convinced that all these incidents aren't related somehow, or tied to her ex. It's even possible that Jack hired this Doug guy to harass me, and eventually Skye. I haven't told her because once I do, she'll think she's safe, and I'm not ready to leave her unprotected yet."

Beck's brows rose. "So, you're lying to her?"

Tripp winced at how that sounded. "More like a lie of omission because I haven't told her I've heard back from Zach yet," he said, then met his brother's gaze, pinning him with a direct look. "What would *you* do if you were in this situation with Chloe?"

"The same," Beck acknowledged. "Trust my gut and do whatever it took to protect her, including lying by omission."

"Exactly." Tripp dragged his fingers through his hair and exhaled a deep breath. "Fuck, I don't know what I'm going to do, because I can't keep this information from her indefinitely. But once she knows it's not her ex, then there's no reason for me to keep an eye on her and stay close by, either."

Beck groaned sympathetically. "God, our women are such stubborn creatures sometimes."

Tripp couldn't argue that, especially when it came to Skye. "Now that I have the guy's home address, I'm going to have to make time when Skye is at work or home in the evening to go to his house and confront him about why he's been following me, just to rule out Jack's involvement." But Tripp also knew that it could take a few days to pin this Doug Hammond down, because he wouldn't necessarily be home when Tripp stopped by.

A low, frustrated growl of sound escaped Tripp. "You probably think I'm being over-the-top neurotic about this situation, but if I wasn't around and something happened to Skye and the baby—" Realizing what just came out of his mouth, he abruptly stopped and narrowed a warning gaze at Beck, whose eyes went wide in surprise. "Skye isn't ready to say anything to the family yet, so you did *not* just hear that."

Beck held up his hands as a slow grin spread across his face. "Hear what?" he asked with feigned innocence. "Although that does explain why you're being so neurotic, as you put it. And just between us, I get it now. I wouldn't take any chances with my wife and daughter, either."

The slider opened at that moment, and the women, and Whitney, came out onto the patio just as Tripp's father and Drew returned with a shovel and bag of fertilizer and potting soil. His mother, Chloe, and Georgia had glasses of wine, while Skye had opted for iced tea.

He caught her gaze and she smiled at him, looking relaxed and at ease with his family.

As soon as Whitney saw her papa and her uncle Drew with a shovel and a big bag of potting soil and fertilizer, her cute little face lit up with excitement.

"I wanna help dig!" she said in a high pitched voice. "Daddy even let me bring my shovel from my garden tools at home!" She raced inside the house and returned with a miniature sized plastic garden shovel in her hand, ready to lend her assistance.

Tripp picked up the bucket with the recently delivered rose bush, and they all headed down to the yard where the other roses had been placed throughout the years. Finding the perfect spot for the newest one, Tripp rolled up his shirt sleeves and with the help of his brothers and Whitney, they planted the shrub.

Then, they all stood back as his mother said a few

sentimental words about her daughter. Tripp added a few of his own, because despite the passing of twenty years, this annual memorial was when he felt the loss of his twin the most and missed what could have been. Back when she first died, this day had been marked with a lot of tears and sadness, but now there were smiles and only the best memories of how Whitney had lived her life so fully in the short time she'd been on earth.

"Everybody hungry for dinner?" his mother asked after they were done.

His brothers were the most vocal about food, and as they walked back toward the house, Tripp slowly followed behind the group with Skye by his side.

She slid her hand into his, shocking him with that display of affection, even though no one was looking their way. He glanced at her, and she treated him to a soft, sweet smile that reminded him of the kiss she'd given him that morning that had felt like a definitive shift between them. Like now, with her kind, caring gaze, and that completely unguarded expression on her face.

"That was beautiful," she said, giving his hand a gentle squeeze before releasing her hold on him, the brief moment severed. "I wish I'd had the chance to meet your sister."

"Me, too," he murmured, knowing that Whitney would have loved Skye as much as he did.

Back at the house, they sat at the dining table as his mother pulled items out of the oven that she'd left there warming and brought them to the table. First, a savory pot roast, followed by glazed carrots, then rosemary roasted potatoes. As each item was set down and the delicious scents of dinner mingled, Tripp noticed Skye shifting in her seat, becoming increasingly uncomfortable beside him.

He glanced at her, recognizing those signs of nausea as she gave him a wan smile, her hand pressed to her stomach as the entrees started circling around the table and everyone started enthusiastically dishing up their plates. When Georgia passed Skye the bowl of glazed carrots, she managed to place a serving on her plate, but as soon as the dish was out of her grasp and on to the next person, her hand fluttered up to her throat and a panicked look flashed across her features.

Concern surged through him as she paled significantly. "Skye—"

"Oh, my God," she whispered in a horrified tone as she quickly scooted out her chair. "Excuse me," she uttered, and bolted down the hall toward the bathroom.

The room went still and quiet, all eyes shifting from Skye's retreating back, to Tripp—sending him varying degrees of concern and shock at her abrupt exit. Clearly, nobody had noticed her escalating symptoms. Well, no one but Chloe, anyway, who had a wise, knowing look in her gaze.

Shit.

"Is she okay?" his mother asked, her worry evident in the tone of her voice.

Tripp placed his napkin on the table next to his plate. "I think I need to go find out."

"No, you stay," Chloe ordered, not giving him a choice as she immediately stood up before he could. "*I'll* go and see how she's doing."

Stunned by his sister-in-law's insistence, Tripp glanced at Beck, expecting his brother to say something to stop Chloe, or to tell her to let Tripp handle the situation, but he didn't say a word as his wife retrieved a bottle of water from the kitchen then followed in Skye's direction.

"Seriously?" Tripp said to his brother, unable to keep the annoyance out of his voice.

Beck shrugged and dug into his pot roast. "I've learned that when Chloe is that adamant, I don't argue or interfere. Trust me, you shouldn't either."

Tripp found it difficult not to go to Skye's rescue, but he begrudgingly deferred to Beck and didn't interfere because maybe what Skye needed right now was a woman's support instead of a man's ineptitude when it came to understanding what she was going through.

Because there was one thing Tripp was fairly certain of . . . Chloe had already figured out what the rest of his family hadn't. That Skye was pregnant.

Chapter Fourteen

S KYE THANKFULLY MADE it to the bathroom just in time to empty the meager contents of her stomach into the toilet. Of all times to finally get sick, she couldn't believe it had been in front of Tripp's family. So damn embarrassing.

She winced as she stood up and made her way to the sink to rinse her mouth and splash some cool water on her cheeks. Now that there was nothing left in her stomach, the worst of the nausea had passed, but she was too mortified to return to the dining room and try to explain what had just happened without revealing she was pregnant. The last thing she wanted anyone to think was that she had the flu or had been repulsed by Audrey's cooking. Yeah, so not cool.

A soft knock on the door startled Skye, and she dried her face with a hand towel, trying to do what she could to get herself back to looking presentable. "I'm okay, Tripp," she said, knowing he was probably worried about her. "I just need a few more minutes and then I'll come back to the table."

"It's Chloe. Can I come in?"

Skye hesitated, surprised to hear the woman's

voice on the other side of the door. On one hand, she wasn't ready to face anyone yet, but on the other hand it had been kind and considerate of Chloe to check on her.

Skye liked Chloe. In the short time they'd been in the kitchen before joining the guys in the backyard, she already felt as though they'd formed a quick friendship. Of course, Chloe had been curious about her and Tripp, and somehow the other woman had asked all the right questions, prompting Skye to reveal that she'd hadn't just met Tripp recently. So, Chloe was privy to the knowledge that she and Tripp had dated when he'd been living in Boston years ago, and that they had recently reconnected.

Another knock jolted Skye out of her thoughts, a persistent Chloe clearly reminding her that she was still waiting for a response.

Skye didn't want to be rude to Chloe when the other woman was just expressing concern, so she exhaled a deep breath, and opened the door, forcing a smile. "Sorry about that. I'm not sure what came over me."

Chloe's perfect blonde brows lifted slightly, as if not quite believing Skye's lie. "How about we sit down somewhere quiet for a few minutes," she suggested, obviously sensing that Skye wasn't ready to return to the dining room just yet. "Come on. Follow me."

Chloe turned and walked farther down the hall, and Skye followed her into what appeared to be a guest bedroom. Chloe sat down on the bed, and Skye settled in beside her.

Chloe handed her the bottle of water she'd brought, and Skye accepted it gratefully. "Thank you," she said, then took a drink, the cool water feeling so good on her parched throat.

The other woman tipped her head to the side, a knowing glimmer in her eyes. "That queasy pregnancy sickness is the worst, isn't it?"

Surprise shot through Skye, and she almost choked on her next sip of water. Oh, Chloe was clever, blatantly calling her out, and while Skye knew she could deny being pregnant, the truth would come out soon enough, anyway. And she honestly didn't want to lie to this woman who had been nothing but open and friendly with her.

"Yes, it is," she admitted quietly.

Chloe nodded in understanding. "Do you want to talk about it?"

There was no judgement or pressure in her voice. Just the offer to be a listening ear if Skye wanted one. "I'm not sure what to say." As much as she liked Chloe, she wasn't at the point where she felt comfortable sharing the details of the baby pact she'd made with Tripp. That was personal and private between the two of them.

"Does Tripp know?" Chloe asked curiously.

Skye smiled, remembering how excited he'd been to see those two lines on the pregnancy test. "Yes. We just weren't going to say anything to the family until I had a chance to see a doctor. And I didn't think today would be the right day to make that announcement, anyway, when it's all about remembering Whitney."

Chloe grabbed her hand and gave it a squeeze. "I can assure you that nothing would make Audrey and Kurt happier than knowing they have another grand-child to look forward to. Today isn't just about celebrating Whitney's life. It's about celebrating *family*, which you are now clearly a part of forever."

Skye's throat grew tight with emotion. Everything was so different with Tripp, his family so warm and accepting and genuine. Jack's parents had been cold and distant, never truly embracing her as part of the family. She'd always felt like an outsider, like she wasn't good enough for their son, but she'd also come to learn that his entire family was dysfunctional and their ambivalence had nothing to do with her.

"But I understand that you and Tripp need to de-cide when the time is right to make the announcement," Chloe went on. "I only just met you, but just know that I'm happy for the both of you. I saw the way that Tripp looked at you the night of the charity auction, and I knew then that you were some-one very special to him."

Skye's cheeks warmed at the compliment. "Thank you."

"The one thing I know about the Daniels men is that when they fall, they fall hard. And from what I've seen between you two, Tripp is crazy about you." She smiled and stood up, not ready to go any deeper with Skye, done with the conversation for now. "I'll let everyone know that you're fine and you'll be out in a few minutes."

Chloe turned to leave, and Skye quickly stopped her. "Chloe . . . will you send Tripp back here?" She'd taken what Chloe had to say to heart, and now she needed to talk to Tripp about letting his family in on their news.

The other woman grinned. "Sure thing. I know he's worried about you, but I kind of asserted myself and told him to sit at the table while I checked on you, which he wasn't happy about. I just thought you might need a female friend to talk to."

"I did," Skye said, smiling. "Thank you."

Chloe left the bedroom, and a few minutes later Tripp walked in, his worried gaze focused on her face. Before he could speak, she did.

"I'm okay, really," she said as he sat down beside her. "But Chloe knows that I'm pregnant and I think we should tell the rest of your family."

He winced. "Because of what happened at the dinner table?"

She laughed lightly. "Yes, because jumping up and running to the bathroom to get sick was rude as hell, and I don't want your mother to think I didn't appreciate the meal she'd made."

He chuckled, then turned more serious. "Is that the only reason? Because you don't owe them any explanation for—"

"I *want* to tell them," she said, taking his hand and intertwining his fingers with hers before exhaling a deep breath. "I know it's still early in the pregnancy, but this kid is happening, and I'd really love for your family to share in our happiness."

"They will love that, too," he said, and pressed a chaste kiss against her temple.

Hand in hand, as a couple, they walked back into the dining room where everyone was mostly done with their meal. As soon as they entered, everyone went quiet and Audrey's warm, concerned gaze went to Skye, but Tripp spoke before anyone else did.

"So, Skye and I have some news to share with the family," he said, taking the lead, as if knowing how nervous Skye was, because this announcement was so momentous.

Everyone waited for him to continue, and the grin that lifted Tripp's lips was filled with pride and legit excitement, leaving no doubt in Skye's mind that she'd made the right choice to have a baby with Tripp. He wanted this child as much as she did, and he was going to be an exceptional father.

He slid an arm around her waist and pulled her close to his side, not bothering to hide how much he cared about her, which brought tears to her eyes at that blatant show of affection in front of his family. She wanted to blame the surge of emotion on pregnancy hormones, but it was getting increasingly difficult to deny the truth, that this man was everything she wanted and dreamed of, but never believed was possible.

"Skye is pregnant," Tripp finally said after leaving

the family hanging for too long. "We're going to have a baby."

"Oh, my God," Audrey exclaimed, tears filling her eyes as she stood up and walked over to Tripp and Skye. Without hesitation, the other woman pulled her into a tight embrace. "I'm so thrilled to be a grandma again!"

Everyone's responses were nothing like Skye imagined they'd be. Sure, they were surprised, but even Tripp's brothers and his father congratulated them with genuine enthusiasm. Nobody asked about their relationship, or questioned if they were getting married—they just accepted the situation for what it was. No pressure or expectations.

Audrey sighed, pressing a hand to her heart. "What a perfect day for that announcement," she said, smiling ecstatically at Tripp. "Your sister would be so happy for you."

"I know she would," Tripp agreed, hugging his mom.

"Mommy!" Whitney shouted, making her little three-year-old self known amongst the chaos that had ensued around Skye being pregnant. "I want a baby, too!"

With a cute smirk on Chloe's face, Skye watched as the other woman glanced at her husband. "I think we can make a baby for you happen."

"Tonight?" Whitney insisted impatiently.

"Making a baby takes time," Beck said, ruffling his fingers though his daughter's silky hair. "But Mommy and I will definitely start trying tonight." He waggled his brows at Chloe, who blushed.

"I want a girl baby," Whitney said, already putting in her order.

The adults laughed at the little girl's innocence, and the rest of the evening passed quickly and they all had a wonderful night.

By the time she and Tripp arrived back at her place, she was mentally and emotionally exhausted, but extremely happy with the way everything had turned out.

She headed into her bedroom to change into something more comfortable, reflecting on the day's events with a smile—as she realized how grateful she was that her child would have the kind of close, traditional family unit Tripp had. The kind she shared with her parents and brothers. There was no doubt their baby would be surrounded by love, no matter what kind of relationship she shared with Tripp. For the first time she felt a spark of hope . . . that maybe, possibly, she could have it all . . . with Tripp.

He was offering her everything she'd ever wanted and dreamed of, if she just had the courage to reach out and take it. He didn't have to articulate his feelings for her, or say what *he* wanted, because from that first night at the bar until today, he'd shown her with his actions how much she meant to him. How badly he wanted to share in her dream of having a baby. And how much he wanted her to be part of his life in every way.

JUST A LITTLE PROMISE

She placed a hand on her stomach, accepting that what he desired for them extended beyond her being his baby mama. Having already acknowledged her feelings for Tripp, at least to herself, it was time to lower her guard and finally let him back into her heart completely.

She put on the sexy, pale gray chemise he'd given her the night at the hotel and strolled back out to the living room.

His eyes widened when he saw her, raw desire darkening his pupils as he took in her seductive attire, but he didn't move from where he was standing by the sofa.

"I know the couch can't be all that comfortable to sleep on," she said, smiling at him. "I was thinking you should stay in my bed tonight." This was the first time she was coming to him aside from their desire to make a baby.

She was breaking her own rules and he obviously knew what that meant to her. Stopping in front of him, she shifted nervously on her bare feet. It wasn't easy to be so open and vulnerable, but it was exhilarating because she trusted Tripp with her heart. He'd *earned* that privilege, and she knew he'd never abuse it.

He groaned at the offer, a deep, growly sound that sent shivers through her. "If I stay in your bed, it won't be to sleep." His gaze never left hers.

"I know," she said quietly. "I want you, Tripp. *All* of you."

She held out her hand, and his green eyes locked

onto hers, as if recognizing that her invitation was a huge deal.

He didn't ask any questions, nor did he pry into her reasons. As always, this man didn't put any pressure on her, or make any demands. He just accepted her offer for the gift it was.

Taking her hand, he led her into the bedroom. By the time they reached her bed, her emotions were at the surface, begging to be set free. She might not be ready to say the words *I love you* to him yet, but she tried to show him, instead.

She stood up on her toes and softly, gently kissed his lips, slow and seductive, and when that wasn't enough and she needed more, she gradually sank a little deeper, sliding her tongue along his. With a greedy groan against her mouth, he skimmed his hand beneath the hem of her gown. At the first heated touch of his fingers along her bare skin, an uninhibited heat pooled between her thighs, stealing Skye's breath and replacing it with an undeniable, soul-deep longing.

No man had ever made her feel so much need and desire, except for Tripp. He was everything she'd ever wanted, everything she craved, and she didn't waste any more time, quickly pulling his clothes away to get him naked. Her chemise ended up on the floor in a heap, and once they were both naked, Tripp pressed her down onto the bed and moved completely over her, both of them impatient for a deeper joining.

His fingers tangled in her hair, gripping the strands tight as he captured her mouth with a relentless

202

passion that seemed to ignite a desperate fire in both of them. He settled more fully between her spread legs, the head of his shaft sliding through the slick moisture already coating her pussy before he pressed insistently at her core.

With a firm thrust of his hips, he drove all the way inside of her, right where he belonged. She gasped against his lips, reveling in the exquisite sensation of him filling her full, and the way his big body shuddered told Skye that the pleasure was equally acute for him.

He ended the kiss and lifted his head to stare down at her face, giving her a glimpse of everything he was feeling, too, as he thrust in and out of her. "You always feel so damn good," he said on a groan. "So fucking perfect."

With him, she felt perfect. So whole and complete.

He moved even faster, his eyes darkening as she gripped his shoulders and tightened her thighs against his plunging hips, hanging on for the ride as he drove her higher. His own jaw clenched as he held back, waiting for her to reach the point of climaxing first, which was already starting to happen.

Her lips parted as her breathing escalated, and her lashes fluttered closed as the delicious tension inside of her loosened and began to unravel.

"Look at me, baby girl," he demanded in a harsh murmur, his own body taut above hers. "I want to feel it all, and I want to look into your beautiful blue eyes as you come for me."

She forced her eyes back open, losing herself in the depths of his hot, vivid gaze just as the last tendrils of her release broke free. Deep and intense, she cried out as the orgasm quaked through her and pulsed around his shaft. Tripp grunted as he buried himself to the hilt one last time, coming right along with Skye as her body splintered into a thousand tiny pieces of heaven and sheer bliss permeated her entire being with equal parts pleasure, and an overwhelming amount of emotion.

When she came down from the high of her orgasm and the adrenaline rush receded, Tripp moved off her and pulled her into his arms—the one place where she knew she would always be safe and secure.

Chapter Fifteen

Monday morning, Skye was in such a good mood, she hadn't argued when Tripp had insisted on following her to work in his car. He felt secure letting her enter the parking garage herself, since the only way a driver could get inside was with a permit that had to be scanned in order to grant a person access.

Once at the office, Skye couldn't stop smiling and over coffee that morning she'd spilled the beans to Lauren about her positive pregnancy test, her weekend with Tripp, and how they'd shared the announcement with his family. Skye had been too excited to keep the news to herself, and she grinned even now when she recalled the way Lauren had screamed in excitement when she'd told her about the baby.

She'd even filled Lauren in about Tripp's suspicions about her ex being in New York. Skye still didn't think it was likely. Sending her a sketched portrait in the mail was one thing, but actually making the long trip from Boston just to stalk her seemed absurd. What didn't seem impossible was Jack finding out about Tripp and turning his anger on the new man in her life. Tripp was worried, and she'd be a fool to completely discount the possibility that Jack was so unhinged.

✧　✧　✧

THE WORK DAY passed quickly and soon it was time to leave. Tripp had called earlier, and Skye assured him Lauren would walk her to her car after work. Skye also promised to send him a text message when she was on her way home, and that she'd meet him there.

They stepped out of the elevator and into the employee parking structure.

Lauren paused and Skye stopped beside her. "Pregnancy definitely looks good on you," her friend said, not for the first time today. "This is the happiest I think I've ever seen you and I'm so excited for you."

"I appreciate it." Skye smiled. "That's probably because it *is* the happiest I've been in years," she admitted.

After her divorce from Jack, she'd gotten to the point where she'd been content, but she never believed she'd feel this much joy again. Thanks to Tripp returning to her life, she could see a wholly different future than the one she'd been determined to live alone. One that included a family and a present father to their baby.

Lauren dug into her purse, retrieving her car keys while casting a curious look at Skye. "Do you think Tripp got any information yet about that car he said was following him?"

"I don't know if he's heard back from Zach yet but I plan to ask him about it tonight."

Lauren gave her a cheeky grin. "At least in the meantime, you have a hot bodyguard staying at your apartment. Nothing to complain about there."

Skye laughed. "True." She pulled her cell phone out of her purse. "I promised to text him once I was in the car."

"Let's get you inside so you can go home and wait for your man."

Skye startled at those words, realizing how true they were. Tripp was her man and she was ready to embrace everything that meant. Her heart skipped a beat. Last night she'd taken the first step, coming to him on her own so they could be together outside of making a baby. Now it was time for her to tell him she was ready for the full, happy life he offered her and their child.

They were three cars away from Lauren's when a dark vehicle turned down their lane, heading in their direction. And it was only because Tripp had drilled the mention of a *black sedan* into her brain, that Skye took extra notice of the car with the tinted windows. A man sat behind the wheel, wearing sunglasses, as he drove toward them.

Though she couldn't see the face of the man or clearly identify him as Jack, unease twisted in Skye's stomach. Intuition screamed at her to get back into the building. Even if she was being paranoid, she'd rather be safe than sorry.

"That car matches the one that's been following Tripp," Skye said, her tone urgent as she grabbed her friend's hand and redirected them back toward the elevator. "We need to get back to the hotel."

Lauren didn't argue or ask questions, just matched Skye's quick strides. But the car continued closing the distance between them with increasing speed, outpacing any progress they made.

Skye's heart raced. Dropping her friend's hand, Skye unlocked her phone and hit Tripp's name on the screen. She knew he couldn't do anything to help her, but she needed to hear his voice, even if only as a recorded sound.

"Hey, baby girl." His affectionate, *real* voice surprised her and she almost burst into tears. "Are you on your way home?" he asked.

"I—" The approaching vehicle slammed on its brakes and screeched to a stop beside them. She sucked in a breath as a man emerged, no sunglasses on now, enabling her to see his entire face.

"It's Jack!" She screamed and turned to run in her high heels. She only got a few steps before an arm wrapped around her waist and wrenched her back from behind, jarring her body and sending her cellphone flying out of her hand.

The device landed on the cement with a loud *crack*, and Lauren stared on in helpless horror as Jack dragged her to the car, swung open the back door, and pushed her into the seat. He shoved her so hard and fast that her entire world seemed to spin. Before she could recover, he slammed the door shut and was back behind the wheel. She jerked backwards as he slammed on the pedal and the car peeled away from the scene.

Adrenaline rushing through her veins, Skye sat up and immediately tried to open the door, prepared to jump out no matter how fast the car was going. But her attempts were futile. Jack had engaged the child safety locks.

She thought about grabbing his hair and yanking hard, but they were surrounded by concrete columns. If he drove into a pole at this high rate of speed, the impact would undoubtedly injure her, and possibly the baby.

"Let me out of this fucking car!" she shrieked.

He slammed on the brakes, the jarring stop propelling her against the back of the front seat like a rag doll. She moaned and grabbed her belly, her first instinct to protect her baby.

Jack whirled, a gun in his hand, aimed right at her chest. "Put on your seatbelt and shut the fuck up," he yelled, the deranged look in his eyes prompting her to obey. "If you make any stupid moves, I will not hesitate to shoot you."

Skye believed him. He'd never pulled a weapon on her before, and the fact that he did so now told her just how insane he was. And how serious he was about this abduction, and her cooperation. And she knew no amount of self-defense moves could stop a bullet from killing her. She couldn't stem the fear overwhelming her, but she was aware enough to realize that she not only had her own safety to consider, but the baby she was carrying, as well.

He'd made his point so she finished buckling up and sat back in the seat, compliant. For now. From her vantage point, she saw he'd placed the gun on his thigh, within reach.

Arriving at the exit to the parking structure, he swiped what was obviously a permit from the dashboard of the car, and the gate opened onto the street. Skye figured he'd either broken into a vehicle and stolen one or he'd forged one, and the extent he'd gone through to kidnap her made her stomach churn.

"Where are you taking me?" she asked, trying to keep her voice calm instead of demanding answers. She had to remind herself that Jack liked her subdued and submissive, fearful even.

While those tendencies rebelled against the woman she'd become, she had to let him believe he was in control so he'd eventually drop his guard and she could find an opportunity to escape.

"I'm taking you somewhere no one will find you," he said, his tone all too cocky. "And somewhere I can talk some fucking sense into you."

"It's kind of late for that, don't you think?" she said, swallowing back her sarcastic tone. "We've been divorced for over a year." Shit. So much for being submissive, she thought.

He glanced at her in the rearview mirror, his gaze

narrowed on her in the backseat. "The only reason I finally signed the divorce papers is because I wanted you to see that I could be reasonable. That I'm not the monster you pushed me into being," he said, sounding rational, as if he truly believed the words he spoke. "I thought giving you time on your own would make you realize what a mistake you made leaving me, because no one else would want someone as damaged and broken as you."

She jutted her chin out, barely reigning in her anger. "I'm not damaged or broken."

"Aren't you though?" he mocked, shaking his head as he merged onto the highway. "You were so pitiful the day you walked out on me."

She balled her hands into fists on her lap, wishing she could pummel them into his head instead. "If I'm so pitiful, why would you even want me back?"

"Because you're mine, Skye," he said, and his voice changed, his tone now the menacing one she remembered and her stomach clenched despite her outward show of bravado. "You'll always be mine and a divorce won't change that. And there is no way I'm going to allow another man to take what is mine."

God, he was so delusional, a true psychopath, and despite her outward show of confidence, she hated that he still had the ability to terrify her. "How did you find out about Tripp?" she asked.

"I've had a PI giving me weekly reports on you since you moved to New York," he said, and shrugged, as if it was a perfectly normal thing to keep an ex-wife under surveillance. "Everything was going to plan until that asshole, Tripp, decided to make a move on you. Or maybe it was you who made a move on him? The PI couldn't really tell. He just said that after meeting him at The Back Door, he took you back to his place and you didn't leave until the next morning."

She sucked in a startled breath. Knowing he'd been watching her for so long, and without her knowledge made her want to throw up.

"The fact that you let another man fuck you *pissed me off*. I was always coming back for you but that pushed up my timeline and I decided it was time to step in." Jack's knuckles turned white against the steering wheel.

"And you think kidnapping me is going to convince me to take you back?" she asked incredulously.

"Maybe, maybe not." He tapped the gun against his thigh and met her gaze once again in the rearview mirror. "I may have to employ *other*, more persuasive tactics. But regardless, it is time for you to come back home and be a dutiful wife."

"That won't ever happen, Jack," she snapped, her demure façade long gone.

"We'll see about that. Apparently I left you alone for too long. You've gotten stubborn and defiant, so I suppose it might take some time to break you down again." He cast a quick glance back at her, and his smile was chilling. "While you've been gone, I've made some additions to our new home, including turning the basement into a soundproof, locked bunker. I figured it would come in handy until you prove to me that I can trust you again."

He really *was* insane and fear rippled through her. What she was hearing seemed so implausible, so over the top and horrifying, but she'd watched enough true crime shows to know that someone like Jack could be capable of doing just that. He'd already shown her his threatening, intimidating, and controlling side, so locking her away somewhere was merely an extension of that depraved personality.

Trying to keep her panic at bay, she stared out the window, praying that someone found her before she disappeared forever. The only thread of hope she had was Tripp. He would *never* stop looking for her. What scared Skye most was what condition she would be in by the time that happened.

Instinct had her wanting to cradle her stomach but she didn't think telling Jack she was pregnant with Tripp's baby was a good idea. No matter what he had planned for her, she would fight to keep her baby alive inside her.

After a long drive, Skye realized that they were in a residential area of Brooklyn, just a few close blocks away from her apartment. Jack turned into a driveway, opened a garage with a press of a button, and parked inside. Once the doors were back down so no one could see them, he ushered her into the house with the gun at her back, giving her no choice but to follow his lead.

"Where are we?" she asked, wondering if this was the new home he'd been referring to.

"This house belongs to Doug Hammond, a colleague of mine who works in the New York offices. He's in Europe for the month, and when I told him I was going to visit a friend in New York, he offered me his place to stay." Jack flashed her an *aren't-I-clever* grin.

"That's . . . convenient," she said, as Jack took her arm and guided her into the living room.

"We'll lay low here for a few days, and then I'll take you to our new home," he said, talking as if kidnapping her was perfectly normal.

She turned around to face him. "You're not going to get away with this," she said, her defiant side emerging again. "Lauren heard me scream your name, so you're the first person the cops are going to look for."

"They won't find me," he said, unconcerned. "First of all, the car and house are in Doug Hammond's name, not mine. As for the home I bought . . . I purchased it under a shell corporation. My identity isn't attached to the deed."

Jesus. Smart and insane were not a good combination.

Tucking his gun behind his back, in the waistband of his jeans, he picked up a long plastic zip tie from the coffee table, where there was also a large roll of duct tape. "Turn around and put your hands behind your back."

Realizing what he intended to do, Skye knew she

had to stop arguing with him and become the agreeable wife he wanted. She needed to show him how cooperative she could be because having her arms restrained would limit her ability to fight or escape if the opportunity arose.

She didn't turn around, but instead placed a hand on his chest and gave him a soft, sweet, docile look, forcing herself to be seductive despite the need to throw up. "You know, it doesn't have to be this way."

He lifted a dark brow, suddenly interested. Being the narcissist that he was, of course he'd believe she still wanted him. "What way can it be?" he asked.

She swallowed back the bile rising in her throat and let a sultry smile curve her lips. "Like . . . old times."

His eyes lit up at the offer. "Prove it," he said.

She bit her bottom lip, all for show. "How about we have dinner first?" she asked, trying to buy time. "Then I'll do whatever you want to prove myself to you."

"Okay . . . I bought some groceries." He took hold of his gun again, removing her ability to reach for the weapon. "Let's go. Kitchen's straight that way." He gestured for her to walk ahead of him and she did as he followed behind, leaving her aware of the gun he held. "As you know, I'm not much of a cook," he said, conversationally. "But I figure a frozen pizza will get us by."

Her stomach roiled . . . from her being captive or her baby rejecting the suggestion of gross cardboard pizza, she wasn't sure. "Okay, that sounds fantastic."

He sat down at a small table in a nook area where he could keep an eye on her. "Go ahead and fix us dinner," he said.

She retrieved the pizza and pre-heated the oven. She opened drawers under the pretense of trying to find utensils and cookware, then ... BINGO. She came across a butcher's block of knives on the counter.

She continued her dinner prep, waiting until Jack glanced down at his phone before palming one of the serrated knives and sliding it into the pocket of her dress. The thought of being caught with the weapon made her as sick as the idea of sliding it into his skin, but she'd do anything she had to in order to survive.

Once the pizza was in the oven, Jack stood back up, leaving the gun on the table as he approached her, and she immediately recognized the perverse glint in his eyes that made dread slide through her veins.

"How much time do we have?" he asked, crowding her against the counter and pinning her in with his hands braced at her sides. "About fifteen minutes before the pizza is done?"

She nodded. "Yes."

He pressed in close, crudely rubbing his erection against her. "More than enough time for you to get on your knees and prove what a loyal wife you're going to be."

Oh, God, she couldn't. "Jack . . ."

His hand shot out and gripped her throat until she

could barely breathe, his eyes blazing with malice. "Fucking *do it*, Skye," he ordered in that harsh, mean tone that had always instilled fear in her. "Or trust me, it's going to end up being much worse for you."

She didn't doubt him for a second, because she'd seen that side of him. "Okay," she wheezed, trying to keep from passing out.

He released her, fully expecting her to obediently drop to the floor and suck his cock. He stepped back, giving her more than enough room to execute her alternative plan. She placed her hands on his shoulders, as if she was going to lift up and kiss him. Instead, she gripped tight, raised her leg, and before he realized her intent, drove her knee fast and hard, straight into his balls, just as Spencer had taught her.

He howled in pain, bending over as he grabbed onto his dick with one hand, while attempting to grab her with the other. His objective was to stop her from running around him but she had stronger goals. Knowing her and her baby's lives were at stake, she retrieved the knife from her pocket and drove it into the side of his neck.

Blood spurted over her hand and chest, and he made a guttural, pained sound, as he tried to reach for and remove the knife, his face contorted in agony and rage. She only had a short window of time to escape and ran for the door, unbolted the locks, and ran smack into a wall of muscle.

She was so disoriented she screamed, but strong arms wrapped around her and she instinctively fought, trying to get free.

"Skye, it's me, and you're okay," Tripp's warm, familiar voice said, holding her tight as she trembled in his arms. "You're okay, baby."

Knowing she was finally safe, Skye broke down and sobbed.

THE SOUND OF Skye screaming Jack's name, then the line going dead, made Tripp's blood run cold and terror grip his heart. He'd just left the office, intending to head toward the address Zach had given him that matched the information on the black sedan's registration to confront Doug Hammond.

Now he was breaking all speed limits to get there as fast as he could because that was the most logical place where Jack would take Skye. No doubt her ex believed no one would make the connection between Doug Hammond and Jack Tremont. And Tripp wouldn't have, if Jack hadn't cut him off the previous Friday, giving him time to snap a picture of the car's license plate.

The man's arrogance was his own undoing, but it also gave Tripp the ability to save Skye. He refused to think of any other alternative. As he raced toward the address, his stomach in fucking knots and trying not to imagine the worst, he called 911 and reported a kidnapping, and gave them the address where he believed Skye had been taken. At least he hoped and prayed that's where she'd be.

He arrived at the house in a nice residential area in record time. Before his car had even come to a complete stop he shoved it into park and leapt from the vehicle, leaving it running as he bolted toward the front door, which was locked. As much as he wanted to pummel his fist on the door, he didn't knock, not wanting to alert Jack that anyone was there to rescue Skye. Assuming they were inside.

Instead, Tripp looked through the clear glass side window next to the door and peered inside. The living room appeared normal. Beyond that was the kitchen and that's where he saw movement. A man fell to the floor, then Skye, racing toward the front door, sheer terror on her face.

Just as he was about to smash in the side window, he heard the locks on the other side unlatching, then the door flew open, and Skye slammed into him in her quest to escape the monster she'd somehow managed to take down.

She screamed, a shrill sound escaping from her throat, and he immediately wrapped his arms around her, hoping to calm her. She struggled against his hold, her fear and confusion palpable as she tried to fight him off.

"Skye, it's me and you're okay," Tripp assured her, feeling her trembling in his arms. "You're okay, baby."

Hearing his voice, she finally realized who held her, that she was finally safe, and her body went limp and huge sobs wracked her body.

As much as he wanted to keep holding her close, he had no idea what had happened with Jack. Tripp could still see him on the kitchen floor, but he'd propped himself up against a cabinet—seemingly immobile, but still a threat, until Tripp knew otherwise. And until the cops arrived, he intended to make sure the son of a bitch didn't find a way to escape.

He gently released Skye, pulling her away from him, seeing the tears streaking her face and the fright still lingering in her eyes. There were splotches of blood on her cheek, arm, and dress, and his gut clenched tight. Tripp was fucking furious at the man who'd dared to kidnap his woman.

"Did he hurt you?" he asked Skye, needing to make certain she was physically okay, because if Jack had harmed her in any way, he was going to pay a very steep price.

She shook her head. "He didn't get the chance." Then, she buried her face in her hands. "Oh, my God, I stabbed him with a knife and I think I killed him!"

Tripp fucking wished that were true. She might have incapacitated the man, but unfortunately, he was still alive from what he could see.

"Everything is going to be okay," Tripp promised, trying to keep his composure for her sake. "But I need you to go and wait for me in the car. Lock yourself inside until the police get here."

Her hands clutched his arms, her frantic eyes on his face. "What about you?"

His jaw clenched tight. "I have some unfinished

business to attend to."

"But—"

He shook his head and Skye's shoulders slumped as she obviously realized he wasn't going to give in. He watched, waiting until she made it to his car and was safely inside, then strode into the house.

Tripp headed straight for the kitchen. Sirens sounded close by, telling Tripp he didn't have much time alone left with this prick to make his point. Up close, he could see how pathetic the other man looked, whimpering like a baby as he pressed a hand to his dick and blood poured from the wound near his neck. His other arm hung limply, making Tripp wonder if Skye had hit a nerve when she'd stabbed him. His chest swelled with pride at her ability to protect and defend herself. *That's my girl.*

Jack had the audacity to glare at Tripp, a sneer curling his lips, even as he slumped back to the floor.

Feeling vindictive and a bit savage, Tripp stepped on the top of the knife still sticking out of Jack's flesh, driving the blade even further into skin, muscle, and tendons. With no strength to stop the attack, Jack screamed like a girl, giving Tripp the immense pleasure and satisfaction he needed.

He hunched down to Jack's level, wanting the other man to look him in the eyes. "It's a fucking pity Skye missed your main artery, you piece of shit."

"Fuck you," Jack spat out weakly.

Tripp gave him a cruel smile. "No, *you're* the one who's fucked. And just know this. If you ever touch

Skye again, or dare to even look at her, or contact her in any way, I will fucking kill you myself. I'm a doctor and trust me, I can make your death slow and excruciatingly painful. If you ever get out of prison, you sick fuck."

He heard cars screeching to a stop outside, indicating law enforcement had arrived, and less than a minute later a dozen police officers swarmed the home and took Jack into custody. Because of his injuries, EMTs were called and arrived to transport Jack to the hospital, but promised he'd remain cuffed, with no way to escape.

At Tripp's insistence, they checked Skye over, wiping the blood off her face the best they could. Thank God she had no external wounds and her vitals were all within normal range. Given the shock and events she'd endured, Tripp was concerned about her pregnancy but she insisted she felt fine and just wanted to go home. The paramedics agreed.

After giving her statement to a law enforcement officer, she left with Tripp. Though she was fine physically, her emotional trauma would take longer to heal. But one thing was for certain. He would be there for her, every step of the way.

Before taking her back to his apartment, Tripp swung by Skye's place so she could pack a bag with her things. She didn't argue when he insisted she stay with him, and he assumed it might be because she was still in shock. But her reasons didn't matter to him. Skye and their child's safety did.

By the time they arrived at his place, she had dark circles under her eyes and her face was pale and drawn. She was exhausted and all he wanted to do was take care of her. To let her know that she wasn't alone and she could depend on him, without fear of losing the independence he knew was important to her.

First, he stripped them both down and put Skye in a warm shower, washing her hair and body as she stood and let him care for her. No need for her to know it was also his way of being able to run his hands over every inch of her skin to assure himself that she was truly unharmed. She didn't seem to mind his attentiveness, or how he insisted she eat something, before bundling her in a warm blanket, sitting down on the couch, and cuddling with her on his lap.

She burrowed against his chest with a soft sigh, and he held her close while stroking her hair. Only then did he really allow himself to process what had happened, and how close he'd been to losing Skye to a deranged madman.

The cop who'd taken Skye's statement told them that Jack would most likely be put away for a very long time. Between the kidnapping, the aggravated assault, possession and use of a firearm, and ignoring the protective order still valid against him, he had a lot of serious charges stacked up against him.

"Move in with me, Skye," Tripp said, breaking the comfortable silence between them. He hadn't planned the words but he meant them.

Yes, he was aware that he was probably rushing

things after what had occurred, but it was that same ordeal that made him not want to waste any more time. He couldn't bear being separated from the woman who was his entire world. He wanted to be a part of her life and their child's life, every single day.

"Okay," she said softly, shocking him with her easy acceptance.

He continued threading his fingers through her hair, wondering if she misunderstood what he meant. "In case you're wondering, I'm not asking you to move in with me because I want to protect you. There's no reason for that any longer. I'm asking because I love you and I want to spend my life with you."

She lifted her head from his chest, her smile so damn sweet. "I know," she replied, her eyes crystal clear as she pressed her palm against his cheek. "I want that, too. You and our baby are my future, and everything I've ever dreamed of. I love you, Tripp, and that's not going to change. I just need you to be patient with me because I need to take things a little slow."

He groaned, beyond grateful and happy with that compromise, and the fact that she finally admitted her feelings. "I'll take you any way I can have you."

He understood her need to take things one day at a time after everything she'd gone through with Jack.

She pressed her lips to his and kissed him, pouring so much emotion into their connection, he knew she'd completely lowered her walls and let him in. No more uncertainties or doubts. Just the kind of love that was always meant to be.

Today was just the start of their lives together. He had faith the rest would come.

Epilogue

Five months later . . .

S KYE GRIMACED AT her reflection in the mirror as she adjusted the form fitting dress she'd put on for her birthday dinner, still trying to get used to her new curves—mainly, her six month pregnant belly that looked like she'd swallowed a basketball, and her very voluptuous breasts.

Tripp walked out of their bedroom closet, and it didn't help matters that he looked absolutely gorgeous in his tailored black trousers and light gray dress shirt. While he'd remained in great shape, she'd already gained sixteen pounds, and there was no denying her hips were a bit wider, too.

She sighed, wondering if she should change into something more flowy, then decided to ask Tripp his opinion. "Does this dress make me look fat?"

Tripp raised a brow at her question, though she could tell he was stifling a chuckle at her pouty question. "No, it makes you look pregnant and sexy as fuck," he said, coming up behind her and sliding his hands around her stomach while burying his face against her neck. "If you need me to prove it, I'm up for the task before we head to dinner."

His amorous response alleviated her worries and gave her that boost of confidence she'd needed. She truly loved being pregnant. Everyone said she "glowed", but being on the petite side, there were days when she felt, well, *big*. And she still had three more months to go.

Resting his chin on her shoulder, Tripp rubbed his palms lovingly over her belly. "How are my two little sprouts doing today?" he asked, just as one of the babies kicked his hand.

She laughed. "Does that answer your question?" She shook her head, feeling another swooping somer-sault happening in her belly. "I'm sure these two are going to be acrobats right out of the womb."

Yes, they were going to have twins—a boy and a girl—and while Tripp was thrilled—and she was, too—he wasn't the one carrying around two rambunc-tious babies.

"Ready to head out?" Tripp asked, stepping away.

"Yep." She nodded and picked up her purse.

They left his apartment where she'd been living for the past five months, and got settled in his car. Once he pulled onto the main street, Tripp glanced at her and smiled, his eyes glimmering mischievously.

"I know we have plans to meet family and friends for dinner," he said, reaching across the console and taking her hand. "But I pushed up our reservation by an hour so I could give you your birthday gift before we meet up with everyone."

She rubbed her hands with excitement. "I can't wait to see!"

She was definitely curious about whatever present he'd bought her, since he'd been so secretive about it.

They drove out of the city, taking the Cross County Parkway, then the Bronx River Parkway and finally she couldn't stand the suspense. "Where are we going?" she asked.

"It wouldn't be a surprise if I told you, now would it?"

She sat back with a pout, paying close attention to the signs. He turned off the exit to Scarsdale, taking some short, winding roads. Finally, he brought the car to a stop in front of a large, empty parcel of land that was surrounded by other high end, custom built homes.

He got out of the vehicle, so she did the same.

"What's this?" she asked, not sure why they were there.

He took both of her hands in his, his excitement tangible. "*This* is where we're going to build our new home and start our future together."

Skye's mouth opened wide, because she knew that a piece of property like this had cost a small fortune, even if his real estate brother, Beck, had gotten him a deal.

Recently, they'd discussed the possibility of buying and relocating into a house, especially once the babies were born and they'd need more room for them to grow, but she honestly thought that decision would be a few years down the line.

"What do you think?" he asked, sounding anxious for her approval.

"I think this is an extravagant birthday present," she said with a laugh but even she heard the happiness in her voice. "But yes, I love the area, *and* the idea of building our own place together."

Relief passed across his handsome features, before he exhaled a deep breath. "Then just one more thing before we start the building process."

She tipped her head. "What's that?"

He reached out and tucked a strand of hair behind her ear, his expression softening as he stared at her. "I want to make an honest woman out of you before our babies are born, so they grow up knowing how much I love their mom," he said, wearing his heart on his sleeve for her. "I want to marry you and make us official and take care of you for the rest of our lives. I need to know you're mine, in every sense of the word. You're the only woman I've ever wanted, and that's never going to change."

She was still reeling from the gift of land and his heartfelt words, when he reached into his pocket and pulled out a black velvet box, getting down on one knee on the asphalt. He popped open the box, and the setting sun shone off the stunning diamond ring nestled inside, leaving her speechless.

"So, Skye Abbott, will you marry me?"

So many emotions gathered in her throat, and she

had to forcibly swallow them back, but her heart was soaring at the realization that all her dreams had come true. Tripp had waited so patiently for her, allowing her the time she needed to heal from the recent past so she could be a better woman for him.

Now, she was so ready to take this next step with him and be his wife and give *him* her whole heart. "Yes," she said with joy, extending her left hand for him to slide that gorgeous ring onto her finger. Happiness overflowed inside her. "Yes, of course I'll marry you, Tripp Daniels."

He slipped the ring on her finger, then stood back up and kissed her—hot and deep and packed with so much feeling she never wanted it to end. This man meant everything to her, and she was so grateful that they'd been given a second chance to get it right.

Thanks for reading! Up next at the bachelor auction: Chase Gossard in JUST A LITTLE CHASE. His heroine is Lauren Connelly, who works for Jade Dare and makes an appearance in JUST ONE KISS!

Other books in the Dare Crossover Bachelor Auction Series:

JUST A LITTLE HOOKUP

JUST A LITTLE SECRET

JUST A LITTLE PROMISE

JUST A LITTLE CHASE

For Book News:

SIGN UP for Carly's Newsletter:

carlyphillips.com/CPNewsletter

SIGN UP for Erika's Newsletter:

geni.us/ErikaWildeNewsletter

Carly Phillips and Erika Wilde Booklist

A Dare Crossover Series
Just A Little Hookup
Just A Little Secret
Just A Little Promise

Dirty Sexy Series
Dirty Sexy Saint
Dirty Sexy Inked
Dirty Sexy Cuffed
Dirty Sexy Sinner

Book Boyfriend Series
Big Shot
Faking It
Well Built
Rock Solid

The Boyfriend Experience

About the Authors

CARLY PHILLIPS is the bestselling author of over eighty sexy contemporary romances featuring hot men, strong women, and the emotionally compelling stories her readers have come to expect and love. She is happily married to her college sweetheart and the mother of two adult daughters and their crazy dogs. She loves social media and is always around to interact with her readers. You can find out more and get two free books at www.carlyphillips.com.

ERIKA WILDE is the author of the sexy Marriage Diaries series and The Players Club series. She lives in Oregon with her husband and two daughters, and when she's not writing you can find her exploring the beautiful Pacific Northwest. For more information on her upcoming releases, please visit website at www. erikawilde.com.

Made in the USA
Middletown, DE
11 March 2024